RANGER

DRAGON BRIDES

KATE RUDOLPH

 Created with Vellum

DRAGON BRIDES

Fated mates, fierce women, and dragon princes are ready to find their mates in the new Dragon Brides series from Kate Rudolph.

Crux
Ranger
Saber

ABOUT RANGER

He's supposed to be a prince, not a prisoner...

Things are as bad as they can get for Ranger when he's thrown in a cell and told he's about to be sold for a profit. But his captors don't know he's a dragon, and he's ready to rain fire on them all in payback.

Until he meets Sidney.

She's stronger than she looks...

When Sidney discovers Ranger on the ship, it throws her world into upheaval. She's no slaver. She'll do what it takes to free him, even if it means crossing her captain and crew. When Ranger turns the tables on her, she's almost too angry to be attracted to him.

Almost.

Freeing Ranger has repercussions. And soon it's not just Sidney that's in danger, but everyone she loves as well. She'll need to trust the dragon prince if she's going to save them all.

But how can she do that without losing her heart?

Fated mates, fierce women, and dragon princes are ready to find their mates in the new Dragon Brides series from Kate Rudolph.

1

Rough hands dug into Ranger's arms, the force barely blunted by the thick fabric of his clothing. He struggled, but it was of little use. The two humans holding him had strong grips, and there were two other humans ready—eager, even—to do him harm if he broke free.

He'd been struggling ever since they caught him.

Stupid. So, stupid.

But how could he ignore a distress call in this corner of space? He wasn't that far from his home planet of Vemion, and he had a duty to help anyone he could save.

Stupid.

"This one's in good shape. He'll catch a fair price." The human trailing them to cut off that escape route made the comment. Ranger didn't bother to try and turn and get a look at him. These humans didn't all look the same, but they all wore the same grim expression that came from a hard life lived on the edge.

"Boar's not going to be happy," the human on his right arm said as he jerked Ranger forward. Apparently Ranger wasn't moving fast enough. "We need to stop home before we hit any of the markets."

They must have been confident about their setup if they spoke so openly. Ranger didn't like that. He had the martial skills required of a dragon prince, but those worked better when he had an army to back him up.

He could tell them he was a prince.

The thought came and went just as quickly. Yes, his father would ransom him without a second's hesitation. Or, if these humans played it right, he'd give them a reward for Ranger's safe return.

But even in a few sentences, Ranger had heard too much. These humans were just as likely to spook and kill him as return him home.

And he'd never hear the end of it if his father knew this had happened.

He was supposed to be on a mission, not trussed up by second rate human slavers and in dire straits.

Well, they might have been first rate. They had captured him without much trouble. Of course, he'd been knocked out by a cheap shot. But that didn't matter.

Ranger's flame simmered within him, but he held it back. He was almost certain these humans thought he was just another human. Humans and dragons looked alike... until a dragon shifted or summoned their flame or warrior form.

Then things couldn't be more different.

But he decided to keep his human form for now. He needed to figure out more of this situation. And he didn't want to give these people a clue to his actual strength. Not to mention the fact that he was exhausted. He hadn't had much of a chance to fight back, but whatever they'd done to him had sapped him of strength. He needed a minute to recuperate.

And if they were dragging him to a cell, he'd have plenty of time.

The matchmaker hadn't warned him about this.

He struggled more as they turned a corner, unable to just give in to what the humans wanted him to do.

Ranger thought back and wanted to curse the dragon woman. He knew his brother had gone to her not long before he disappeared from the palace. His father was uncharacteristically quiet about Crux's whereabouts.

So Ranger had taken it upon himself to find his older brother.

The matchmaker was the best clue, especially

since she didn't answer to the king. Not directly, at least. Everyone answered to the king eventually.

She'd given him instructions to head into space and follow his instincts.

Now he wondered if this was a setup. Was the matchmaker working with these humans and taking a cut of the profits? Slavery was strictly prohibited in Vemion, and slavers were dealt with harshly. But that didn't mean people didn't try.

Ranger was a fool.

He jerked his arm and caught the human at a weak moment. He broke free and lashed out, elbowing the man in the face and making him cry out with pain as bright red blood burst from his nostrils.

Ranger heard a satisfying crack and smiled, even as the other humans piled onto him and paid him back three times over for his act of defiance.

His lip was split and his eyebrow cut. He was sure to have a black eye. But his nose wasn't broken. He spit blood onto the walkway.

The humans gripped him tighter and picked up the pace.

He didn't have time to fight back again.

Ranger tried to get his bearings, but there wasn't much to see. They were on a ship of some kind, cargo if he had to guess. Cargo ships could be like mazes, and if this one was normally used to transport slaves, he wouldn't be shocked if it was full of secret hideaways and hidden hallways.

He should have been paying attention to their path rather than wallowing in his own failure.

But what was done was done. And he'd made one of the humans bleed. He could at least be proud about that.

It was only a few minutes and two turns later that the humans brought him to a stop in front of a door. The human leading their group placed his palm against a scanner and the door slid open.

He stepped aside and let Ranger's two guards shove him into the dark room. Ranger stumbled, and before he could turn around, the door was already sliding shut.

Ranger burst into action and slammed his fist against the door. Unsurprisingly, it did nothing. His anger wanted him to pound against the door until his hands turned bloody and he made a dent.

But a smarter part prevailed.

He let his hands fall to his sides and breathed deep to steady his heartrate. Panic wouldn't gain him anything except a headache. He was a dragon warrior prince. He was above panic.

His racing heart didn't seem to realize that.

He couldn't hear anything outside of the cell. The humans could be standing right outside waiting to see if he had any tricks they hadn't yet seen. Or they could be on their way back to wherever they normally dwelled on the ship.

If Ranger was a betting man, he'd guess the latter.

He looked around. The cell was dark, but there was just enough light to see by coming from recessed lights in the wall. He'd never loved the dark, so he was thankful for that small blessing.

He looked for a camera or any other surveillance equipment but didn't see anything. That didn't mean it wasn't there, but for now he was willing to take his chances.

He took a deep breath and called on his warrior form, feeling a knot of tension uncoil as his skin thickened with scales and claws grew out of his hands. Now that he had a moment to think, he realized just how panicked and disoriented he'd been while the humans dragged him here.

His warrior form could have made quick work of four humans.

And yet he'd hesitated.

Stupid, useless prince.

But he was here now and could only move forward. He tested the door with his claws, but they barely scratched the metal. He was stronger in this form, too, but he couldn't put a dent in the door.

Fire was his only hope.

It was dangerous on a ship. He didn't know the oxygen content of the air around him. If it was too much, he could end up making a fireball that destroyed the ship and left them dead in space.

Better dead than enslaved.

Ranger summoned his fire, but rather than breathing it, he let it flow into his hands until they glowed red hot, then he set them on the door.

He heard a strange hissing, and for a moment thought the door was buckling under the heat.

Then he yawned.

His eyes felt heavy.

He could barely lift his arms.

He caught sight of some sort of gas coming from a tube on the floor right before the strength went out of him and he fell to the floor, unconscious.

2

Sidney banged her wrench against a pipe and cursed as water shot out. "Wrong one, wrong one." She glared at the makeshift water treatment machine. It was older than her and made up of more rust than actual parts. The water in the settlement had a distinctly metallic taste, and the chemical tests that Sidney ran every week were coming back more and more toxic as time passed.

They needed a new machine. Or she needed to figure out magic so she could fix this one with nothing but spit and hope.

If the toxicity levels weren't bad enough, the machine was working at half capacity and dropping. They wouldn't have *any* treated water if it kept up.

"Making headway?" Cyclone peeked her head into the shed where Sidney was working.

Sidney jerked in surprise and almost slammed her head against one of those rusty pipes, pulling back just in time. She wasn't concerned so much about a concussion as what *she* could do to the pipe. Rust had a habit of breaking easy.

"Depends on how much toxic metal you want in your water. Or how much water you want." She had to scoot on her ass to get untangled from all the pipes, and only when she stood up did she notice just how stiff her muscles had gotten. Lovely. She followed Cyclone out of the shed and rolled her neck, trying to work out the kinks. "We need to replace the filtration system at the least. It would be best to replace the whole machine."

Cyclone gave an uncaring shrug. "Water tastes good enough to me."

"You can't detect dangerous toxins by taste. Mostly." Sidney tightened her grip on her trusty wrench and resisted the urge to chuck it at the water treatment machine.

Cyclone just rolled her eyes. She was one of the settlement elders, a woman that Sidney had looked up to for all her life. She had long gray hair she kept in tight braids and wrinkled pale skin that was starting to look as gray as her hair. Sidney wasn't sure how old Cyclone was. She'd been an adult all of Sidney's life, but it was scary to consider that the woman was getting *old*.

"Don't know why we need some fancy machine," Cyclone muttered again.

It was an old argument, one Sidney didn't feel like having right now. She'd started working on the mechanical equipment with her old mentor a dozen or more years before. Now she was twenty-six or so and the only person who cared about maintaining the equipment that kept their settlement running.

They'd carved out a bit of land for themselves on a barely habitable planet. It was the only home Sidney had ever known, even if she hadn't been born there.

She knew she had to be grateful.

But it could be frustrating to scream about how the settlement was on the verge of disaster and no one seemed to care. After all, everything had been fine for years.

They didn't mention that in those years a mine had been dug upstream from their town and all the runoff and refuse polluted their water. Sidney was the one who had to care about that.

And she wasn't going to argue now. Cyclone couldn't help her.

"Boar's landing," Cyclone said as they walked from the water treatment station down to Shadow's to grab a bite to eat for the midday meal. Half the town was lined up out the door of the restaurant, waiting for whatever Shadow had put together. She had a way with cooking that everyone else in town envied.

"I thought the crew was gone for the month." Sidney tried not to let excitement overtake her. Boar had listened to her last time she talked about repairs. The money wasn't there, not yet, but he understood the concern. He'd told her he'd bring it up to the council.

Maybe he'd listen about the water treatment machine.

She and Cyclone shuffled through the lunch line. Shadow moved fast, and it only took about ten minutes to get their food. They took it to one of the nearby trees and sat in the shade.

"Don't know why he's back soon," Cyclone said as she munched on her stew, scooping up the thick liquid with bread.

Sidney ate fast. She'd been pulled away from too many meals by breaking equipment, and she wasn't letting a bite of Shadow's stew go to waste. And eating gave her a few minutes to think.

"Do you think something's wrong?" she asked between bites.

Cyclone shrugged. She'd served on the settlement council for years before her retirement, but after she'd stepped back, it was like she stopped caring about the goings-on of the settlement. She talked with who she wanted to talk to, she went where she wanted to go, and she didn't let herself worry about what she didn't control.

Sidney wasn't sure if that was admirable or not.

She'd just finished the last bite of her stew when Prodigy, one of Boar's trusted lieutenants, ran up to her. He had a bandage on his nose and nasty looking black eyes.

"Are you okay?" she asked before he could greet her. "What happened?"

Cyclone just looked at him with one eyebrow raised.

"Some cargo wasn't properly stored." Prodigy winced as he spoke, and his tone was more nasal than usual. "Boar wants to see you. Now."

Sidney didn't make him wait. She bid farewell to Cyclone and followed Prodigy to the edge of town where the landing pad for their ship was located. The ship was too big to land on the planet, so they used a ferry to travel to and from space.

She couldn't remember the ship. She'd only been on it once, back when she was an infant, rescued from a wreck and taken in by the settlement. Sidney didn't think of it much, she was far too busy. But heading towards the ferry brought back memories.

The ferry was three times as tall as a person and as big as the gathering hall in the center of town. If this was *small,* Sidney could hardly fathom how big the ship up in space was.

Boar was waiting for them at the launch pad. He was a giant of a man, easily a foot taller than her, with huge muscles and a bushy beard. He was in his forties, or maybe his fifties by now, and until he'd taken over the space missions a decade before, he'd been one of the adults charged with her care.

Sidney didn't have adoptive parents, that wasn't how the settlement worked. Children were raised collectively. She only knew the other way because she'd been able to read old Earth books that were kept in the settlement library. Their ways sounded strange.

"Go get your nose tended to," Boar told Prodigy as they approached. The other man turned around and headed back towards the settlement without another word. Strange. Sidney would have thought they could treat something as simple as a broken nose on board. But Boar didn't give her time to question. He slung a friendly arm over her shoulder and gave her a hug. "It's good to see you, girl. It's been far too long."

Sidney hugged him back. "You're the one who keeps flying away."

Boar laughed. "You know it's necessary."

That's what everyone said. It was easier to fly through space to the other side of this planet to buy supplies than to trek over land. And the other planets in the system were densely populated. The settlement wasn't self-sufficient. They had to hire out the ship for any number of reasons to keep the settlement going.

Speaking of. "We're having trouble with the water treatment machine." Boar wasn't in charge of the settlement or anything, but he did have the ear of the council. He was likely to take a seat the next time one came open. If anyone could help her, he could.

"Are we now?" He let her go, and they walked towards the control building on the edge of the launch pad. No one was there. The place wasn't occupied except for when the ferry was coming or going.

Sidney explained about the contamination and flow issues, and Boar seemed to listen, but when she was done, he just sighed.

"Sounds like an expensive problem to fix," he said.

"We do need parts. Or a new water treatment system." Sidney couldn't say how expensive anything was. They didn't use money in the settlement. They had some, she knew, from their missions, but it was allocated to the settlement's needs. All the citizens were easily provided for.

But judging by the look on Boar's craggy face, it was more expensive than they could afford. "I can't have us going hungry to replace a machine I know you can fix."

For a second, the words warmed Sidney, but just a second. "I don't know if I can fix it. And if it breaks, we'll be drinking poison." She wished she had her trusty wrench right now, if only for how comfortable it felt in her hand.

Boar met her eyes with a determined gaze. "You're a genius, kid. You can do it. When you get back."

"Back from where?" The water system could go at any minute, and things were always breaking around the settlement. Sure, Sidney wasn't the only one who knew how to fix up a machine, but some days it felt like she was the only one who really cared.

"Claw got herself hurt on the last mission. We need a mech to finish the job, and you're the girl I need. Pack a bag, we leave at nightfall." He clamped a hand on her shoulder. "You've got this. And if all goes well, we'll have more than enough resources for a new water treatment machine."

A hundred objections threated to pour out of Sidney's mouth. She didn't know how to take care of a ship. She'd never been out of the settlement. She had a hundred things to take care of at home.

But Boar was already walking away, and the words were caught in her throat.

And under it all was excitement.

She'd never left the settlement. But now she was going to *space!* She'd get to see things she'd never dreamed of.

Sidney took off running back towards her house. She had a bag to pack and a galaxy to explore.

3

WHEN RANGER WOKE UP, his head weighed at least a hundred pounds more than it usually did. His brothers often called him arrogant, but he didn't think that had anything to do with his current situation. He wished it was arrogance swelling his skull.

Unfortunately, his memories were clear. He didn't even have a second to wonder where he was.

On a slaver ship, in a cell, barely conscious after a bout with knockout gas.

He forced himself to his feet. There was no one in the room with him, and there was still that dim illumination from the recessed lighting.

He could see. The gas was gone. He was awake. These were good things.

But not good enough. He was never going to hear

the end of this if he had to be rescued. He hated to think how much Crux would rub his face in this... forever.

And he didn't trust that rescue would come soon enough. His brothers were fierce warriors, but they had no idea he was here. Crux was off planet, and Saber probably didn't know Ranger was gone. By the time anyone knew he needed help, he'd be long gone and possibly dead.

He had to get himself out of this mess. Soon.

He'd shifted back to his regular form well in his sleep. No claws, no armor, completely defenseless. It took concentration to hold the warrior form, so he wasn't surprised, but he didn't like to think of how exposed he'd been.

Had something been done to him while he slept?

He shuddered at the thought. But he focused on his body and nothing felt strange. His limbs all felt normal. There were no sharp pains or any issues outside of bodily fatigue, which he attributed to the gas. Though he wasn't sure that anything *would* feel out of place if the people who had captured him had done something to him.

Ranger put it out of his mind. If something had been done to him there was nothing he could do now. He wasn't hurt. He didn't have a collar around his neck. And both of those things could change at any moment.

He had to try and get out now.

Pain hammered at his head, but he did his best to ignore it. It would hurt a lot more if he became someone's slave.

He didn't want to be a slave. He would never let himself be owned.

It hurt to summon his warrior form, but he pushed through the pain and embraced it as his claws grew and his armor thickened his skin to protect him. It was worth the struggle.

He took his anger out on the door again, but just like the first time, it didn't budge. He let out a yell of frustration and wished he was strong enough to bend metal.

But he hadn't had the chance to test fire against the door before being knocked out. And his fire burned hotter than normal.

Ranger summoned white hot flames to his hands and pressed them against the door where he thought the handle should be. If he could weaken the locking mechanism, maybe he could get out.

But his hands didn't seem to do anything except make the door warm, no matter how hot his flame.

Ranger cursed and backed away. It would take a lot of energy to use up all of his fire, but he didn't know if he was going to be fed or tortured, and he wanted to conserve as much of a strength as he could. For now. He'd reconsider if things became dire.

Well. More dire.

He studied the wall again. He didn't think his room was on an exterior wall of the space ship. It would be too much of a risk to leave prisoners potentially exposed like that.

Most transport ships kept sleeping quarters as far into the interior of the ship as possible to guard against potential loss of life from hull breaches. Without any other information, Ranger had to assume that he was somewhere on the inside of the ship.

He would die if he had to, but escape was his first choice. Escape or death. Either was better than slavery.

Rather than try the door again, Ranger summoned his fire once more and worked on the seam in the wall, hoping it was a weak point. The wall started to glow red as his hands worked their magic, and Ranger let out a bark of relieved laughter.

Yes!

This was going to work. He was going to get out. And he was going to get home.

He just had to kill a bunch of slavers and steal their ship first.

4

IT TOOK Sidney a little while to get accustomed to the ship. She was full of apprehension as she boarded and was led to the crew accommodations. She didn't have her own room, and she wasn't sure who she was sharing with. The ship was big, but the crew still bunked together at least two to a room.

Her room was empty when she got there, but she figured she'd see her roommate eventually.

Boar led her around the ship and showed her where she would be working and where the crew hung out when they weren't busy. But he promised they were busy a lot. And as they walked around, it began to dawn on Sidney just how far from home she was. It was exciting.

And terrifying.

Sidney wanted to take her tools and go down to

the engine room and get to work, but Boar assured her that everything was in working order for now, and she could take the rest of the day to get accustomed to the ship.

Then it was time to take off, and Boar left her to go talk to the pilot.

She strapped in to one of the many chairs that lined the halls as the ship took off, but it wasn't nearly as exciting as taking the ferry from the planet. The ship was already in space, so there was no need to break atmo. They didn't rumble and jerk around. She barely realized they were moving and only knew to get out of her seat when the all clear alarm sounded.

While Boar was busy with the rest of the crew, Sidney got up and started investigating. She had never been on the settlement's ship before, not as an adult, at least. She figured this might've been the ship that rescued her when she was a baby, but she didn't know and she hadn't thought to ask.

Sidney wandered the halls until she started to hear voices and followed them until she spotted people. She waved at Challenger and Hog, two of Boar's crewmembers, and they both did a double take when they saw her.

"What?" The question popped out of Sidney's mouth. "Boar brought me on as the mechanic since Claw is sick." She would have thought Boar would mention that to the crew, but maybe the illness was sudden.

Hog had the most doubtful look on his face that she had ever seen, but Challenger gave her a friendly smile. "I suppose it's good to have fresh blood on board. Are you finding your way around alright?" She gave Sidney half of a hug and left her arm around Sidney's shoulders as she led her down a hallway that Sidney hadn't intended to go down. It was in a different direction than she had been walking. "Have you seen the mess hall yet?" Challenger asked.

Sidney hadn't seen *anything* yet, but she was afraid if she said that, Challenger would offer a full tour, and Sidney wanted to figure the ship out on her own. "Not yet. I figured I'd wander around for a bit and find that when I get hungry." She was too nervous to eat right now. Though she was curious about what kind of food they served on a spaceship.

Still, Challenger urged Sidney down the hall. "You should come see the mess. And I'm sure we can find you a map of the ship. We wouldn't want you to end up accidentally throwing yourself out the airlock." She laughed at her own joke. Sidney didn't find it funny.

For some reason it made Sidney a bit uneasy. Not that she was worried about doing that. The airlocks were incredibly obvious. "Other places I'm not supposed to go? Boar didn't say anything about that." She was a mechanic. She had to have access to everything. If something broke in a restricted area, she would need to go fix it. It wasn't like she was planning to steal anything or sabotage the ship.

Hog grunted, and Challenger shot him a nasty look. Then she turned back to Sidney. "No secrets," she promised in a tone that all but guaranteed there were secrets. "We just don't want you to get lost. Here's the mess." They came to a large door which led into a room lined with long tables full of crewmembers.

"Are there specific meal times?" Sidney asked. That was something Boar had failed to mention.

Challenger shrugged, as if that was some kind of answer. "There's usually food in the mess all the time. And a lot of crew like to gather here when they're not on duty. Or when they're not busy. But we announce meal times over the speakers. You won't miss out." Someone called Challenger's name, and she gave Sidney another half hug and walked away to go greet them. Hog went with her.

Sidney considered staying in the mess and trying to eat something, but her nerves were still getting the better of her, and she didn't want to end up throwing up her first meal on board. She could always come back later.

She turned to exit the mess, but her weight was

blocked by Crow, another crewman, a man her age who had grown up in the settlement school with her. "What are *you* doing here?" His tone was not inviting.

Sidney bristled. What was it with everyone? From the way Boar had talked about her joining the crew, it had seemed like this would be something simple. Instead it felt like people were closing ranks. Did she have to expect to find something nasty in her bed? "I'm the temporary mechanic. Claw is sick." Did they not know that? Had Boar kept it secret for some reason?

Crow glared at her, and Sidney wondered why. What was wrong with these people? Why were they acting so strangely? They were all residents of the settlement. She should be just as welcome as any of them.

Crow gave her a cold nod and walked off without a goodbye.

Before Sidney exited the mess hall, she heard somebody at one of the tables speaking. "The merchandise will fix all of our problems. We sell him, and we have a stack of credits as tall as the ship."

Sidney looked over, but she couldn't tell who was speaking. It sent a chill down her spine.

Merchandise?

Him?

There were no slaves in the settlement. Sidney had heard about the practicem but it was barbaric.

But it was the first place her mind went. That's what happened when someone used the words *merchandise* and *him*.

But maybe they were talking about animals or toys or something far less sinister than selling people. She hoped so.

She rushed out of the mess, unwilling to listen to more and start worrying about random snippets of conversation she heard.

She didn't even have a guarantee they were talking about anything real. What if they were talking about a book? Or a media show? She could always ask Boar if the ship was carrying any merchandise. He would tell her.

Sidney headed for the mechanic's office and fired up the monitoring equipment. Sure, Boar said she didn't need to work until morning, but she wanted to get a feel for her job. There were sensors all over the ship that fed into her equipment and would tell her if anything was wrong before things got too serious. This was the best place to map out the ship if she wasn't going to do it on foot.

At first all seemed well, but once the monitoring equipment was completely online, she was surprised to see an excess heat alert coming from the cargo area.

"What are you doing there?" she asked the alarm, as if it could answer. As far as she knew, there was nothing in the cargo holds that generated heat, and since they were not breaking atmo, there was no reason to worry about a heatshield failure.

It was probably a faulty alarm. Boar had mentioned something about that being an issue sometimes.

That didn't mean that Sidney could ignore it. Either the alarm needed to be checked out or there really was an excess heat issue.

She grabbed a heat retardant suit and slipped into it before making note of where the alarm was coming from.

It was time to get to work.

5

RANGER'S whole body ached from the process of breaking out of his cell. But he was making progress. Real progress.

His claws were bloody, and unfortunately it was his own. Every time his heat weakened the cell wall, he scraped at it, but his skin was beginning to tear away, and he didn't know what would give out first, his body or the wall.

It had to be the wall. He wasn't going to let all of his effort be for nothing.

But he had to take a break.

He let his fire fade away and shifted back to his man form, no more claws, no more armor. It was very hot in the cell. He was fire resistant, but not fireproof, and eventually even he wouldn't be able to stand all of the heat.

But he had a while to go until that was a problem. He wouldn't worry about it until his skin cracked and darkened from fire damage.

Ranger traced his finger over the seam. It was bigger, several inches across now, and he could see into the hallway. No one was out there. And apparently no one could tell what he was doing.

He had been at it for more than an hour now, he thought. There was no way to tell time, but he was familiar with the aches in his body from training and campaigns he'd been sent on as a warrior. He knew what it was to hurt.

Eventually he would trip up some sensor or someone would come down into the room and figure out what he was doing. He planned to be out of the cell before that happened. And if he was really lucky, he'd be able to take out his rage on whoever came to investigate.

The fire that lived within him sparked to life at that. He wanted to burn this place to cinders.

He hoped the ship was big enough to hide in, and he would find an escape pod or something to get out. It wasn't a great plan, but at least it was *something*. In a situation like this, he couldn't get hung up on a multistep strategy. He just had to focus on the task ahead of him and get it done.

And that meant break time was over.

Ranger shifted back to his warrior form and

called his flame once more. He lost himself in the work. And the small crack in the seam became a larger crack, until finally it was wide enough that his shoulder could fit. He had to ram it a few times to make sure his entire body could maneuver through.

And with a bit of a scrape against his armored flesh, he was out.

He wanted to fall to his knees and thank whatever god was looking out for him, but before he had even a moment to celebrate, footsteps slammed down the hall and a figure in a bulky silver suit turned his way.

"Stop right there. Who are you?" The voice from inside the suit sounded feminine, but it was coming through a voice box and slightly mechanized. Ranger didn't know if this was one of the people who had thrown him in the cell or one of the other crewmembers of the ship.

He would have turned and ran, but the hallway terminated right behind him, and the only way out was past the person in the suit.

He didn't waste time answering. He charged at her, claws out and ready to fight.

But his work against the cell had tired him out, and he was slower than he should have been. He reached out to hit the woman, but she was surprisingly fast and dodged his punch.

Then she managed to sweep his legs out from

under him.

Ranger was impressed despite himself. But he jumped back to his feet before she could press her advantage. They traded blows, and it became clear very quickly that the first sweep had been a lucky one. This woman wasn't a fighter. She managed to defend herself as well as any civilian might, but Ranger was going to win.

He didn't know if she knew it yet, but he was certain of it.

And he was done playing games.

He summoned his flame and shot it at her, but she dropped to the ground in an incredibly impressive dodge. Something sputtered through the mechanized voice box, but she must have hit it and caused it to malfunction, because he couldn't understand a word that she said.

His fire roiled within him, ready to burst out once more, and it felt stronger than usual, as if there was some kind of force tampering with it. Ranger didn't know if it was the drugs that had been forced on him or if it was his anger at the situation, and at the moment he didn't care.

He dug deep. He didn't care if a fireball caused the ship to explode with him on it as long as it took out everyone who had tried to enslave him. And this time, he wasn't going to miss.

He aimed for the woman and let his fire rip.

6

SIDNEY WAS sure that this strange alien was going to kill her.

She wasn't a fighter, even if she had learned a few moves from some of the kids she'd grown up with in the settlement. And she was angry. This was her first time off of the settlement, her first time in space as an adult. And she was supposed to be going on an adventure. She wasn't supposed to be killed by some strange alien who had stowed away.

Had he stowed away?

The distraction almost killed her, and when the alien sent a wave of fire her way, all of her anger bubbled up, and it felt like she shot it out of herself and at the fire. Somehow the fire retreated and hit the alien, making him slam back into the wall.

Her eyes went wide in shock. Sidney didn't know

what was going on. What had he done? Had *she* done that? How?

She was worried that she'd killed him, but he was groaning against the wall and she had to press her advantage.

She ripped off the helmet of her suit. The voice box was shot, and it was difficult to breathe. Now that she wasn't looking at him through a visor, she could see that he almost looked human, though there were strange plates on his skin as if he were somehow armored, and his hands were covered in claws.

"Are you trying to kill everyone on the ship, including yourself? Who are you? What's going on?" The questions poured out, and the alien—the man—blinked up at her in confusion.

Sidney wished she had a blaster or some kind of weapon so she could threaten him. She didn't know if she could fight off his fire powers a second time, and she hated to think of the kind of damage they would do to the structure of the ship.

"How did you do that?" His voice was scratchy, and some part of her wanted to give him water.

But she wasn't going to tend to the aches of the man who had almost killed her, not at least until she had half an idea of what was going on.

"You have twenty seconds to answer my questions and tell me who you are before I ring the alarm." She should have wrung the alarm as soon as she saw him. If Boar found out that she hadn't, he was going to rip her a new one. Sidney wasn't one to break the rules. Not really. But the conversation she had heard in the mess and the strange way people had been acting was still at the forefront of her mind. Was this man 'the merchandise'?

"My name is Ranger," he said, clearing his throat. "And your crew captured me."

RANGER WAS SHAKING WITH SHOCK. This woman had directed his fire. It should have been impossible. Only a very strong dragon or his fated mate was capable of doing that. And this woman was *not* a dragon. She was human.

A beautiful human. Her hair was held back, but a few dark strands fell in her face and her eyes were wide and fierce. She might not have been a fighter, but she had the heart of one. And his cock was definitely paying attention, even if this was exactly the wrong moment to find her.

His declaration seemed to freeze her in place, and Ranger used that to his advantage, slowly getting to his feet. He didn't know who this woman was, even if signs pointed to her being his mate. Even if she was, he couldn't trust her.

His cock thought otherwise.

His cock needed to take a break.

"They captured me," he repeated. "And I think they are in the process of selling me into slavery. You look surprised." Her fierce expression had morphed into confusion, but not shock.

She opened and her closed her mouth a couple of times before turning away with a curse. "We don't sell people. Slavery's wrong. Boar would never do that." She seemed to be saying it more to convince herself than to convince him.

Ranger could say something mean at the moment. He was the one who'd just been locked in a cell. But the woman seemed genuine. She truly believed what she was saying.

Or possibly that was just his body trying to believe that she could be his.

"What's your name?" He wanted to know it almost more than he needed his freedom.

"Sidney," she said quietly. "My name is Sidney Storm."

"Sidney." He repeated it. He liked the shape of the sounds on his tongue. "Will you help me get out of here, Sidney?" She had just been fighting him. He had thought he might have to kill her. But with the strong possibility that she was his mate, now he could not lay a hand on her, and he would stop anyone who tried.

"This is a big misunderstanding." She was shaking her head and took a step back to put some space between them. "I'll talk to Boar. He'll clear this all up. Maybe they thought you were threat?" She looked at him hopefully.

He almost wished he could give her that comfort. But there was no misunderstanding. "They attacked my ship. After sending out a distress call."

"You were in distress?" Her eyes widened.

But Ranger had to shake his head. "I *answered* their distress call."

Sidney's shoulders slumped. "Okay, that sounds bad." She took a deep breath, but whatever she was about to say was cut off by footsteps down the hall. She looked at him, eyes wide. "Hide," she commanded.

There wasn't any place to hide in this hallway other than his cell, and with the wall destroyed, it would be very obvious that something had gone wrong.

Sidney turned to face the mouth of the hallway, her body doing its best to block his from sight.

But the steps faded away, going in the other direction. They weren't about to be discovered. Not yet.

But soon.

"I'm not going to let anybody sell you into slavery," Sidney promised. But let's find you a place to hide. And then I'll find a way to get you off this ship. Okay?" She looked like she meant it.

"Okay," Ranger agreed.

He didn't tell her that when he left the ship, she was coming with him.

7

Sidney felt… weird as she left Ranger to find a hiding spot of his own and went to find Boar. She was more aware of her body than she'd ever been, and a crazy part of her wanted to turn around and see if Ranger tasted as good as he looked.

Yeah.

Crazy.

It wasn't like she'd never experienced attraction before. She had. The settlement wasn't *that* small. But it had never come up on her this fast. The second the fighting stopped, she'd become aware of just how much her body wanted him. And it grew every second.

They were apart now. Why wasn't it abating?

Sidney took a deep breath and forced those thoughts to the back of her mind. Ranger was new, the situation was strange. This was just a reaction to the sudden upheaval of her life.

She hadn't even been on the ship a day.

This couldn't be real.

Maybe she could have convinced herself of that if she wasn't wearing the heat retardant suit. Ranger had managed to claw it up a bit, another sign of how close she'd come to annihilation.

He could have killed her.

That was another reason for her to slow down on the attraction front. But her body didn't seem to care.

She heard voices and tried to school her expression into something neutral. Then she realized it would all be useless if someone saw her in the fire suit. She ducked down a hallway and got out of the suit before looking for a place to hide it. Luckily there was a closet that seemed to be filled with empty containers and an old mop. No one would be looking there for a while.

Sidney ran her fingers through her hair, trying to make it look a little less mussed. Helmet head wasn't a good look. Her clothes were rumpled from being under the suit, but she doubted anyone would notice.

She needed to find Boar.

Did he know about Ranger? Was he responsible for Ranger's capture? Or was this—hopefully—some big misunderstanding?

She didn't have a good feeling about that.

They'd been sailing through space at top speed for a few hours by now, so Sidney doubted that Boar would be with the pilot. From what she'd heard from people who had flown with him before, he took a hands-off approach to navigation.

That meant Sidney was left wandering the halls and looking for their leader.

She passed by Challenger and gave what she hoped was a friendly wave. Hog was nowhere in sight. But she walked on quickly, in case Challenger got any ideas about having a conversation. Sidney was too close to the edge of cracking up. She needed to find Boar and she needed answers.

Sending out a false distress call to capture someone was a classic slaver move. There was no mistaking it for anything but what it was.

Was Sidney on a slaver ship right now?

She needed an explanation. Or a time machine. If she could go back in time a couple of hours to before she walked down that hall to see Ranger escaping, she would have never known. Then it wouldn't feel like her insides were all tied in knots.

But that was a coward's wish.

She knew now. Or, at least she had reason to believe that something was wrong. Forgetting it, ignoring it, made her complicit.

She remembered where Boar's quarters were on

the map that she'd seen, and his door was open when she passed by. He was alone.

Perfect.

She knocked on the doorframe and Boar gave her a friendly smile. He didn't look like the kind of person who captured others and sold them for profit. But she had no idea what that kind of person actually looked like outside of the caricatures that showed up on media shows.

"Come in, come in." He waved her inside and was the same warm man who'd had a hand in raising her. "How are you settling in?"

Sidney almost closed the door. The questions she had to ask were best kept private. But *if* Ranger was telling the truth, she didn't want to be trapped in a room with a slaver. They were in the depths of space. She couldn't exactly escape. But if she could get out of the room, she could hide.

She didn't trust Boar.

It knocked her for a loop. She'd always trusted Boar. He'd been one of her favorite teachers growing up. He'd taught her how to dice vegetables when she was barely big enough to wield a kitchen knife.

But Ranger's fierce voice was ringing in her ears.

"Something wrong?" Boar asked.

Sidney realized she was frozen in the doorway with a blank expression. She forced herself to smile, but stayed where she was. She didn't want that door closing. "Sorry, been a long day."

Boar made a laugh of agreement. "And it's longer still. We're in range of a local planet and will be stopping there before long. We should be docked for a full day, and you'll have time to take a look around. Your first new planet, isn't it?"

He knew it was. And Sidney wished she could be excited. This was supposed to be exciting. But all she could think about was Ranger. Something, probably good sense, stopped her from making the direct accusation. If Boar was a slaver, he wouldn't tell her outright. Not until he was sure she was loyal to him.

But maybe he'd tell her something else.

"I have a weird question." She was stumbling her way to something that might give her answers and remembered the snippet of conversation she'd heard in the mess.

He leaned back in his chair, still smiling. "Shoot."

Right. How best to say this? "I was wondering about the ship… and the settlement's financial situation. You said we couldn't afford the new water treatment system until this mission was over, but I haven't seen any cargo. What are we hauling? And how does…"

"Money work?" His smile shifted to an expression she'd never seen on his face before. At least, not since she was a child asking stupid questions and getting on every adult's nerves. "It's different out here. Sometimes I wonder if we should start using money in the settlement, just to make everyone understand."

Why did that send a chill down her spine?

Sidney smiled, as if Boar was making a joke, and pressed on. "I heard someone say something about merchandise. I just wanted to know what we're... merchandising?" That was definitely the wrong word.

"We sell all kinds of things," Boar said, as if Sidney were four years old. "And sometimes we haul things from one part of space to another. And we carry... passengers." Something caught in his throat when he said that word.

And Sidney was suddenly sure that Ranger's accusation was correct. Not that she'd really doubted him. After all, he was on the ship.

But she had to keep pushing. "Are there any passengers on board now?"

Boar looked at her for a long moment, and Sidney was afraid that she'd given herself away. But after a bit, he shook his head. "No. Not on this leg."

"I hope we pick some up." She tried to sound as cheery as possible. "It would be fun to meet people from other parts of the galaxy. What planet are we headed for?"

"Kalyx IV."

"I look forward to seeing it. But I'm going to try

and catch a nap before we land." She faked a yawn and hoped it looked real. "I don't want to pass out the second we dock."

"You do that." He wasn't smiling at her anymore, but Sidney hoped he wasn't suspicious.

She backed out of his office and headed to her room. She needed information about Kalyx IV.

She walked down the hall, and suddenly it was like the crew had multiplied by ten. Challenger and Hog were there, along with several others whose names she surely knew, but couldn't conjure at the moment. Had they all just filed out of the mess?

Sidney wasn't in the mood to talk to anyone. And she was worried that Ranger would be discovered. How good was he at hiding? How many places were there to hide?

Her room was a sanctuary. And it had a computer full of information that could give her a hint about why they were really going to Kalyx IV. Sidney didn't think it was to see the sights.

She brought up the information page about the planet and scanned it. There was nothing interesting. It was a relatively populated planet with four major cities and a total population of just under a million intelligent life forms. There was a short list of cultural locations for tourists and a longer lists of restaurants and entertainment locations.

And the bottom of the page noted that Kalyx IV

accepted the practice of slavery and held slave auctions in one of the four cities: Kalyxia.

Sidney would bet the new water treatment machine that was where they were headed.

She didn't know how much money they would get for Ranger, and she didn't want to find out. She wouldn't be tempted. The thought of selling people made her sick. But there was a small part of her that feared she might feel… guilty.

Was this the true source of the credits the settlement needed? Had Boar gone out and captured some unassuming person for a profit every time she begged for new machinery? How much of this was her fault?

She wished she could say none, but she just didn't know.

Sidney needed to find a way to get Ranger off the ship before they landed in Kalyxia. She was certain that if she didn't, he was doomed.

8

A WARRIOR DIDN'T HIDE.

Ranger snorted at his own stupidity. That kind of thought belonged in the head of someone who'd never seen battle. Sometimes hiding was the best tactical move. And sometimes it was the only way to survive.

A very *cramped* way to survive. At first he'd stuffed himself into a closet to keep out of sight, but every time he heard a clank or a groan coming from the ship, he was sure he was moments away from discovery.

The closet he'd chosen had a hidden panel in the back, and he'd managed to wedge himself in and hide behind it. It was getting hot, and he feared he'd run out of air before long, but he wasn't moving until he had no other choice. Or until Sidney found him. Though he wasn't sure exactly how that would work.

He let his mind drift. It was another skill he'd learned as a young warrior. More than half the job was waiting, and he couldn't afford to be bored.

It occurred to him that he should worry about Sidney reporting his escape. She'd even threatened it before he told her what her crew had done to him. But he wasn't worried. She was his mate, she wouldn't turn him in.

His thought surprised a rueful laugh out of him. She had no idea that she was his mate. And he still wasn't completely convinced it wasn't some strange fluke.

But he'd seen the look on her face when she realized her crew profited from slavery.

She wasn't going to turn him in.

Had she given herself away?

He didn't know how long he'd been wedged in the tiny compartment. It felt like hours, but that could have been his mind playing tricks. He wasn't about to give up hope on her just yet.

If her crew had turned on her, he would come for her. It wouldn't be easy to mount a rescue, but she wouldn't be their victim.

He heard the clatter of footsteps and held his breath. He'd sealed up his broken cell as best he could so it wasn't as obvious from the outside that he'd broken out, but he doubted it would convince anyone for long.

The closet door opened, and Ranger wished he had enough room to shift to his warrior form, but it was too cramped.

"Are you in there, Ranger?" Sidney whispered.

He let out his breath and pushed against the panel blocking him from view. "What gave it away?" He'd thought he'd hidden well.

She scrunched up her brow and tilted her head to the side. "Gave what away?"

"My hiding place?" He put the panel back into position, fiddling around with it until he was satisfied all was well.

Somehow, Sidney looked even more confused. "I just... um... well, there are only so many closets a person could hide in." She didn't sound convinced.

"Did you check the other closets?" He rolled his head and shoulders, thankful to have a bit of space to move.

And her eyes followed him through every moment. Then she blinked and shook her own head, as if clearing her thoughts. "No. No, this was the first closet I checked."

Fated mates sometimes had an innate sense of each other. If they really were supposed to be together, she might have sensed him. It was terrifying. And a bit exhilarating.

Mates were relatively rare. Ranger had never expected to meet his, and certainly not after her crew had abducted him.

But he wanted more time with her, time to be sure of the bond, before he said anything or got her hopes up. He didn't want to imagine what his father would say about the match. King Venin was a traditional sort of dragon.

Sidney would not be a traditional dragon bride.

But Ranger was flying far ahead of himself. She'd guessed where he'd hidden. It wasn't magic.

"We're getting close to a planet called Kalyx IV, do you know it?" Sidney spoke quickly and quietly, like she was worried about being overheard.

Of course she was, every minute on the ship brought them closer to discovery. "I'm aware of the Kalyx system," he said. "We're not terribly far from my home planet." He could call for help. These humans wouldn't stand a chance against a fleet of dragons.

"Okay, good. I think Boar plans to sell you in the city of Kalyxia. There's a slave market there. But you're not going to be on the ship when he comes to get you." Now she was grinning.

"I'm not?"

She beckoned him down the hall and stopped. "Escape pod. It's meant to be used if something goes wrong on the ship. Life support lasts for up to seven days and there's some limited flight capability. We're close enough to Kalyx IV for you to land your escape pod safely." She pressed a button and a door slid open to reveal the pod.

Plenty of room for two.

"What about you?" Ranger wanted to tear through the ship in a rampage in revenge for what had been done to him and to keep Sidney from harm. But he wasn't sure she'd appreciate knowing that.

She just shrugged and then forced a smile. "Don't worry about me. I can take care of myself."

It was probably even true. Ranger could step into the escape pod and be on Kalyx IV in no time. He could leave Sidney behind and forget all about crazy thoughts of a human fated mate and his father's disapproval.

But he wasn't going to do that.

Not when his destiny was standing right in front of him.

And it was payback, of a sort. Her crew had kidnapped him. Now he was stealing her.

Ranger put a hand on Sidney's arm and pulled hard, tugging her into the escape pod. She let out a cry of surprise, but there was no one around.

She struggled. It shocked him for a second, but only a second. Of course she would struggle. After all, he was kidnapping her.

She'd thank him later.

He refused to do anything that might actually hurt her. He just needed her restrained until the escape pod was free of the ship.

He got an arm around her and pushed her up against the far wall, holding her in place, their bodies pressed flush against each other. It felt good. So good. And now was *not* the time to dwell on it.

Not even when she breathed deep. Not when her tongue darted out to lick her dry lips.

He wasn't about to kiss her.

He wasn't crazy.

"Let me go," she pleaded.

"No." He reached behind him and pressed the escape button. The door slid closed and then they were off, rocketing away from the ship and towards Kalyx IV and safety.

9

SIDNEY HAD BEEN ANGRY BEFORE, but never like this. Rage fired within her, and she wanted to lash out at Ranger and make him pay. She'd do it, too. As soon as he stopped holding her against the wall.

Why was it so hot in the escape pod?

She really didn't want to *like* how it felt to have his body pressed against hers. Especially since the fire breathing brute was *kidnapping* her.

It didn't matter that her ship had done it first. Sidney had nothing to do with it.

And she wasn't going to let this monster push her around. Or press her in place. She gathered up her strength and shoved Ranger away. He only backed up a step, but it was enough to break his grip on her and let her shimmy away.

But the escape pod wasn't big enough for both of them and her anger.

"What in the name of the most fiery stars are you doing?" she demanded, voice dripping with vitriol. She wanted to hit him, but she, unfortunately, knew just how good of a fighter he was.

Ranger didn't look a bit repentant. "You weren't safe with your crew. Not after helping me."

She hated to think he might have a point. And there was no way in hell she'd admit it. "I get to decide what's safe. You can't just *steal* people."

"That didn't stop your captain and his cronies." Now Ranger's voice shifted to something harsher. "You're lucky I'm trying to save you."

"Save me? Right. Because I need saving from the only people I've ever known. They saved *me*. I could have explained this." Maybe. Probably. Sidney wasn't a troublemaker. But *surely* someone would understand. It wasn't possible that every single person on that crew was okay with selling people into slavery.

Ranger might have answered, but the escape pod rocked, and they each fell back towards the nearest wall. "Strap in," he said. "We're in for a rough landing."

That was almost guaranteed, and it was something Sidney couldn't argue. The escape pod rocked, and Sidney had trouble getting her belt buckled. The turbulence had her hands flying all over the place, and she couldn't properly brace herself in her seat.

Ranger didn't have any problem.

The bastard.

But she finally managed to secure herself right as the turbulence kicked up a notch. They hit the atmosphere and it got hot. Hotter than the fire Ranger had shot out of his hands. Sidney was sure she was going to die, and she wanted to curse Ranger again.

She didn't let herself think about how using the escape pod had been her idea, even if she'd never intended to be on it.

And then the heat evaporated like it had never been there, and Sidney's limbs were heavy as true gravity took over. They were through the atmosphere and free falling.

She was going to die.

Ranger's fingers brushed hers, and then he gripped her hand. Sidney held on tight. In that moment, he wasn't the man who'd kidnapped her. He was the only person left in the universe, and he was going to die right along with her.

Except they didn't die.

Something, maybe a parachute, maybe some mechanism in the escape pod—Sidney didn't really care right then—slowed their descent. Her ears popped as they fell, and it didn't take long before they landed with an almost gentle thud.

The pod didn't have any windows, so Sidney didn't know what kind of environment to expect. Truthfully, she wouldn't know how to interpret much of the environment even if they did have windows. She'd spent her entire life in the settlement. She'd never seen a city or a desert.

Her world was very small.

Until now.

Ranger let go of her hand and unbuckled himself. And then, for some reason, he reached over as if he was going to help Sidney get out of her own seat. And that's when Sidney remembered that she was mad at him.

"Keep your hands off," she snapped, and was thankful when she managed to undo her restraints competently. It would have been mortifying to tell him off only to immediately need help.

Ranger pressed a button beside the door and a computer voice spokc. "Analyzing exterior environment. Please wait."

An engine hummed deep in the escape pod, and the speaker beeped every few seconds as if it was reminding them the program was working.

"Environment satisfactory to life. Air acceptable. Temperature upper range. Precipitation none. Proceed with caution. A beacon has automatically been activated for your safety. Help may arrive shortly." The voice cut off.

Ranger swore so creatively that Sidney didn't recognize most of the words. "Why didn't you tell me to disable to beacon?" he demanded when he ran out of curses.

"How was I supposed to know about the beacon? It was my first day on the crew!" And what a long day it had been. Sidney couldn't remember the last time she'd slept, and exhaustion was starting to weigh her down.

She could stay with the escape pod. She realized it, but she wasn't sure if it was what she wanted. She could concoct a story, say that Ranger broke out of his cell and then kidnapped her when she tried to call for help. Boar might even believe her.

But they'd want to know where Ranger was. And they'd probably try to kidnap someone else.

Ranger studied her, and Sidney wondered if he knew what she was thinking. If he did, he didn't say. "We're getting out of here. We need to get as far from here as possible before your friends come looking for us."

Us. Sidney didn't scoff, but it was a close thing. They'd be looking for Ranger. She didn't even know if anyone realized she was gone.

But they couldn't stay in the escape pod all day,

and once they were somewhere safe, Sidney would be happy to see the back of Ranger for good.

He opened the door, and they both squinted at the bright sunlight streaming through. The air smelled fresh and clean, and Sidney breathed deep. They hadn't had air that smelled this good in the settlement in years.

"Come on." Ranger tugged her out the door. He surveyed their surroundings, and Sidney wondered if he saw something differently than she did. She saw a bunch of trees in the distance and some hills in another direction. They were in a field of tall green grass and the sky was greyish-blue overhead. She didn't see a city, but she heard engines in the air and looked up to see three different aerial vehicles heading in one direction.

Ranger saw them too and nodded in that direction. He grabbed onto Sidney and tugged her a few feet before she thought to resist.

She yanked her arm back and winced as she upset something in her shoulder. "I'm not coming with you. You're free now. Have a nice life."

Ranger made a sound in the back of his throat that Sidney refused to think was kind of hot. "We're not splitting up. Let's go." He stepped towards her as if he was going to pull her his way again.

Sidney stepped back. She was tempted to run, but

there was something about Ranger that reminded her of a predator. And predators loved to chase.

And she didn't want him to start using his fire powers again.

"What are you?" She realized she only knew his name. He was an alien. He had to be. Or maybe some sort of modified human. But he wasn't *normal.* He wasn't like her. "How did you do that fire thing?"

That stopped him in his tracks. "I'm a dragon," he explained, as if that was the most obvious thing in the world.

"You're not a dragon." Sidney wanted to laugh, but he didn't seem to be joking. She'd read enough stories and watched all the media shows in the settlement's library. She knew what dragons were, and none of them were hot guys.

Kidnappers. None of them were absolutely non-hot kidnappers who *didn't* make her think sexy thoughts.

Sidney's brain hurt with the twisted logic of her own denials.

"I'm not?" Ranger held his hands out and looked down at his body. "I think I would know my own kind. How would a human know otherwise?"

"How do you know I'm human?" Sidney wanted to call the question back as soon as she asked. He was going to think she was stupid.

"You're more—" Whatever he was going to say

was cut off by a burst of light and sound coming from behind them. "Take cover!" Ranger dove for her and rushed them both back to the escape pod.

Sidney's back was against the metal of the pod before she could blink. "What's going on?"

"Blaster fire from the east. We can't stay here." He dared a glance around the pod and was met with more shots. He closed his eyes, and Sidney watched in amazement as his skin thickened, seeming to grow some sort of scales, and his hands grew claws. This was what he'd looked like the first time she'd seen him; it was how she'd known he was an alien.

Maybe he really was a dragon. Maybe there was a lot she didn't understand.

How did he look hot even now?

"We're making for the trees. Less chance of capture if we can hide." He studied the path, and Sidney studied him, feeling like a helpless child.

"What happens if they capture us?" She didn't want to know, but had to ask.

"Nothing good." He gave her what she thought was supposed to be a comforting nod, and she was captivated by his eyes. His pupil was vertical, almost like a snake's. It should have looked terrifying.

It didn't.

"Then let's not find out." She sounded braver than she felt.

"Don't stop until you reach the trees," he warned. "Not even if I fall."

"Then don't fall." There were people with blasters out there, and they were up to no good. Sidney didn't want to lose the guy with fire powers. She didn't let herself think about how she'd been planning to walk away from him a few minutes ago. That wouldn't do her any good.

At Ranger's word, they ran, and Sidney kept her eyes on the trees. Looking for the shooters wouldn't do her any good. She almost lost her resolve when the dirt beside her burst as it was hit by blaster fire. Then she sped up.

The shooters could hit the dirt all they wanted, so long as they didn't hit *her*.

She gasped in relief as she stepped into the shade of the trees, but it was still several more steps until she was behind cover and in the woods. She heard Ranger grunt and finally turned to look for him.

He was right behind her and grimacing.

"Were you hit? Are you hurt?" Her heart was beating fast, and she wanted to get her hands on him to check for wounds. She stepped close, trying to get a look.

The blaster shots stopped.

"I'm fine," Ranger said.

They stared at one another for several seconds. Sidney needed to take a step back. Instead, she couldn't stop looking at Ranger's face. His mouth was open and his lips were red. He was breathing a bit heavily, but nowhere near as hard as she was.

And he was alive.

She was alive.

They'd outrun blaster fire and survived.

She reached out a hand and touched his arm. His armored skin was hard under the cloth.

She needed to back away.

Ranger sucked in a breath.

She stepped close and kissed him.

Ranger's arm went around her and pulled her flush against him. His mouth opened, and his tongue swept against hers. Sidney moaned at the contact, her body on fire with desire and the elation of survival.

His kiss was a storm of passion, and she never wanted it to let up.

She was in trouble.

10

RANGER COULD KISS his mate for days and never grow tired of it. She sighed into his embrace as if she were made to be there, and Ranger felt like a king. He'd give up any crown so long as he could have her.

His cock strained in his pants, and he wanted to free it, to lay his mate down and claim her in celebration of their survival.

His claws traced gently down her back, and he remembered he was in his warrior form. If he wanted this to go further, he should shift back, but he didn't trust their attackers to let up just because he and Sidney had cover.

When blaster shots rocketed through the trees, he hated that he was right.

He pulled away reluctantly and couldn't tear his gaze from the dazed look on Sidney's face. He'd kiss her again, he promised himself. And she'd look just like that.

Then she seemed to come back to herself and shoved at him, taking a step back and wiping at her mouth. "You *kidnapped* me. What are you doing?" she demanded.

Now was not the time to remind her that she'd kissed him.

"Take cover," he warned. He was done playing with their attackers. It was time to make them regret their actions.

He stepped out of the trees and let his fire burn bright in his gut before letting it out in a scream that scorched the grasses around them and flattened everything in sight except the escape pod. Ranger could have melted that, too, if he really worked at it, but this was a show of force, and the huge burst of fire was much more impressive than a bit of melted metal.

The planet around them was startlingly silent except for the crackle of fire. Then Ranger breathed deep and called the fire back to him. It left blackened land in its wake as he breathed it in and extinguished his destruction.

He could let his fire rage, but he only wanted to stop the attackers, not burn the planet to cinders.

He stood in the open, arms out and waiting for

another shot of blaster fire. He wasn't behind cover. A single shot could take him out.

But no shots came.

Good.

He didn't think he'd killed whoever was after them. His fire could only reach so far. But he'd shown them that he and Sidney weren't easy targets and they wouldn't be good prisoners. For now, that was the best he could do.

He stepped back into the woods and found Sidney waiting for him, wide eyed and shaking. "You're a freaking dragon."

Now she believed him. But was she scared?

He wanted to kiss her again, wanted to assure her that nothing in the universe could induce him to hurt her. She was his mate.

Most likely.

He could test the theory right here, shoot flame and ask her to direct it. If she could, there was no question about what she was to him. But when she'd done it on the ship, it had been a survival instinct, and he wasn't sure she'd be able to do it consciously.

Ranger didn't want her to fail. He didn't want to find out that she wasn't his mate. He wanted to claim this woman and take her home with him. He wanted her to sit beside him as a dragon princess. He'd fight his father to keep her, or he'd do what it took to keep her, even if it meant walking away from his title.

But he was getting ahead of himself.

It was only one kiss.

But what a kiss it had been.

More kisses had to wait until later. They were far away from civilization, and her people could chase after them at any moment if they detected the distress beacon from the escape pod. And there were people with blasters out there just waiting for helpless victims to stumble into their path.

Ranger didn't like Kalyx IV. He wanted to go home.

He was tempted to change form and fly himself and Sidney to the nearest city, but his dragon form was flashy and likely to call too much attention to them.

"Glad you believe me." Ranger grinned at her and released his warrior form as he shifted back into a man. "Are you going to run away again?"

Sidney shook her head and swallowed, her throat working hard. Ranger wanted to run his tongue along it and prick her with his teeth.

Not yet.

But his cock was eager.

He had to focus on business. For now.

He'd show her plenty of pleasure as soon as they were safe and she had wrapped her mind around the situation. When they next kissed, she wouldn't push him away.

"I can send a call to my people," he said. "But we'll probably need to find a city to get a strong enough communicator. Let's get moving. I don't think we want to be stuck out here after dark."

She walked beside him down a path between the trees. "Do you think there are monsters or something?"

She sounded so worried that Ranger was a bit embarrassed at the laugh it startled out of him. "What? Flesh-eating monsters that only come out after dark? Doesn't sound likely."

Sidney shuddered. "Thank the stars for that. One less thing to worry about."

But after she'd said it, Ranger couldn't stop worrying about it, and he picked up his pace. Sidney didn't complain, she just walked faster right beside him.

This planet was unwelcoming enough as it was. He didn't want to find out what threats lay out there after dark.

11

"WE SHOULD TAKE a rest before we get into the city." Ranger came to a stop at a small building. They were on the outskirts of one of the cities of Kalyx IV, and there were dozens of aliens around them. No one paid any attention.

Sidney was trying not to gape.

Humans were the only people that lived in the settlement. Boar had told her fantastical stories of tricksy aliens and warned her not to trust them unless he or one of the settlement elders had given the okay. But none of these aliens seemed that dangerous. Not unless disinterest was something they had to worry about.

"I could use a rest," she admitted. She had no idea how long she'd been awake, but it had to be more than a day at this point. She was trying not to yawn. She didn't want Ranger to think she was weak.

But she was about to fall asleep on her feet.

"Over there." He pointed to a small, shaded alcove with a nice bench that looked like paradise.

Sidney used her last burst of energy to get to the bench, where she sank down and her bones seemed to melt. "I'm never getting up," she confessed.

Ranger's laugh passed over her and made her hair stand up. He was dangerous, just like Boar had warned. Sometimes he had claws and he could shoot fire. Of course she should be cautious.

But her lips still tingled from their kiss.

Ranger hadn't brought it up, and Sidney didn't have the nerve. Maybe he didn't want a human kissing him. Maybe he was horrified that someone related to his captors had tried to kiss him. She didn't know, and she was too tired to have the conversation now.

"Sleep," Ranger told her. "I'll keep you safe."

She probably shouldn't trust him. He could betray her in payback for his capture. He'd already kidnapped her.

And then he'd kept her safe from the mysterious blaster wielders.

Sidney drifted off without any more resistance.

Her dreams were a muddle of images and scenes

that she couldn't understand, and deep in her heart something blazed red hot.

She woke with a start and realized that Ranger was jostling her. "We need to move." He didn't sound concerned, but his face was serious.

"How long did I sleep?" She felt stiff and dirty.

"Not long enough. The patrol has done a few rounds and they've been looking at us suspiciously. If we can find a credit terminal in the city, I should be able to access my accounts and get us a place to stay overnight." He opened his mouth to say more, but abruptly shut it.

He was thinking about whatever came after a good night's sleep. He had to be. And he didn't want Sidney to know. She could demand. But then he could refuse. Things were going well now, and she didn't want to fight.

Was she walking further into her own abduction? Shouldn't she be worried about getting home?

She was too tired to worry overmuch at the moment.

"Will you have enough credits? How much does it cost?" Not that she could help him if he was short on cash. It sounded ludicrous, needing to pay for a place to sleep. There was plenty of room on this planet, why couldn't they just make do? But that was her settlement logic talking. Ranger understood credits, and for now Sidney would need to trust him.

And for some reason, her question made him grin. "Oh, I think we'll make do."

They continued their trudge to the city and entered through a gate that proclaimed KALYXIA in large, glowing letters. The slaver city. This was where Boar had been planning to sell Ranger.

If he found Ranger, he still might be able to do it.

But Ranger wouldn't go down without a fight. With his claws and his fire, he could kill Boar without a second thought.

Sidney's stomach churned. She hated what Boar seemed to be doing. She wanted it to stop immediately. But she didn't want him *dead*. He'd cared for her all her life. He'd trusted her to help keep the settlement's machinery running. He'd read stories to her and carried her on his shoulders when she was a tiny little thing.

It was hard to reconcile that with his monstrous actions.

"Something wrong?" Ranger asked, glancing back at her.

Sidney realized she'd stopped walking and was just staring up at the city entrance. "Are you planning on killing Boar?" She was a terrible person for caring, wasn't she? If Boar was a monster, didn't he deserve to die?

Ranger stepped back and put a hand on her shoulder. "I'd be happy to never see him again. I have no plans to chase him across the galaxy in revenge. But if our paths cross... you do understand he'll capture more people, don't you?"

She pulled in a shaky breath, trying not to sob. Then she nodded. She couldn't quite manage speech just then. She understood. That was why it hurt.

"You're tired, let's find a place to sleep." His hand slid down until he could lace their fingers together.

It felt nice.

She should probably pull away.

She didn't.

Ranger led her through the city with the kind of confidence that made her wonder if he'd been there before. Then he made two wrong turns and shot her an apologetic look as he turned around and led them back to the main street.

Then Sidney heard Boar's booming voice and squeezed Ranger to make him stop. They were walking right towards Boar. She pulled Ranger back until they were in the shadows of a nearby alley.

"What?" asked Ranger.

"Boar." Her hands would have been shaking if she wasn't holding on to Ranger for dear life. He made her feel safe for some reason she didn't understand and didn't want to examine too closely.

A moment later, Boar, Crow, and Hog came into view. Boar led the two of them, a dark look on his face, his shoulders hunched over. He walked with purpose and headed straight for a building with no sign on its door. However, there was steady traffic in and out of the place, so it was probably a business of some kind.

"I want to know what they're doing," she told Ranger. She wasn't asking permission.

But he gripped her hand tight enough to bruise to hold her in place.

Sidney let her hand go limp, an old trick Boar had taught her. Then she pulled, and Ranger let go in shock. "I'm going."

"You're not going to like what you see in there," Ranger warned.

"What else is new?" Sidney crossed the street, and Ranger followed after.

There was no one at the door to stop them from going inside. The place was crowded. At first Sidney thought it was some kind of performance space. There was a large stage with a white screen behind it, and people milled around on the floor in front of the stage.

"The auction will begin shortly," a voice announced over a loudspeaker.

Dread settled in Sidney's stomach. She doubted they were auctioning knick-knacks. She spotted Boar and the others near the stage and shrank back into the shadows, Ranger right there with there.

"You don't need to watch this," he said. His arm came around her and he hugged her close.

"I need to stay." There was a tremble in her voice, but Sidney didn't let it break her. "I need to see this."

Ranger didn't argue anymore. Sidney didn't pull away.

And several minutes later, a tall blue alien led another alien in chains onto the stage, and the white screen lit up with information about the prisoner.

Boar, Crow, and Hog were at a slave auction. All of Ranger's accusations were true. And Sidney's life was founded on blood.

A tear rolled down her cheek as everything she knew was ripped away. She didn't know what she was doing next, but she had to find a way to make this right.

12

RANGER WANTED to get Sidney out of there. Standing in the room made his skin crawl, and he was ten seconds away from shifting into his warrior form and burning the place to the ground.

This was where he would have ended up if Sidney hadn't found him. He'd be chained on the stage and sold to the highest bidder.

Maybe.

He might have still managed an escape. His claws and fire were more than sufficient to take out a human. But Boar and his crew probably had a few tricks up their sleeves. He saw Boar greet a few other attendees in the audience. The three humans were comfortable in the crowd, and they'd certainly been there before.

Now was the time to make their exit. Sidney's

former crew wouldn't be distracted forever, and Ranger didn't want to rely on a bit of shadow for cover. But every time he tried to turn Sidney towards the door, she resisted, planting herself in place and refusing to move.

Wonderful.

There had to be fifty people in the room, and not all of them were free. Some of the audience members held leashes attached to aliens who stood or knelt quietly beside them. Ranger could murder the room in a single burst of fire, but he didn't want to kill the chained up victims who had no choice in being here.

Fighting forty or so slavers was not a winning proposition.

They really needed to go.

So, of course, Sidney wanted to go deeper into the room.

"What are you doing?" Ranger demanded. He admired his mate's courage, but this was bordering on lunacy.

She glared back at him. "Boar is up to something. If he's not selling you, is he selling someone else? Was there another captive on the ship that I missed? Or is he *buying* someone? I can't let him get away with this!"

"And what are you going to do? Everyone in this room might come to his aid if you interfere." Ranger had enough training to know when battle was the wrong choice. And that was certainly true now. Sidney was riding high on emotion and exhaustion. She wasn't thinking clearly.

But he couldn't force her to walk away.

"We get close," he told her. "But just to listen. If we need to interfere, we do it elsewhere. Got it?"

Her eyes blazed, and Ranger could feel an answering call in his inner fire. But she nodded.

Good.

No one paid attention to them as they slowly crossed the room. A few attendees bid on the alien on display, and then someone won and the alien was taken off stage. Another would take his place soon enough.

He and Sidney were holding hands, and Ranger was glad of it. Focusing on Sidney and her pain was enough to keep him out of his own head and imagining what it might have been like to be led in chains.

No. He had to keep his mate safe. And to do that, he had to focus.

They turned their backs once they were close to Boar so he wouldn't see them, and Ranger put himself between Boar and Sidney. If Boar was going to recognize one of them, it was likely to be her. But they were close enough to hear everything he said.

Sidney stiffened when a new voice entered the

conversation. He spoke with a different accent than Boar and probably wasn't part of his crew.

"I thought you'd have merchandise to trade today. That was our agreement," said the man.

"Eon, you know I'm good for it," Boar said with false bravado. Even Ranger could tell he was lying, and he'd never truly met him.

"I gave you an extension last time," said Eon. "And you took on even more debt."

"It's an expensive business, keeping my people alive."

"Then perhaps I should take them off your hands."

"What?" Ranger tried to glance over his shoulder to see if Boar was about to start a fight, but he couldn't see anything besides the man's shoulder and the shadow of Eon.

"Last chance before our arrangement changes," Eon warned. "And I need collateral."

"Excuse me?" That came from one of the other crewmembers standing beside Boar.

Eon didn't speak to anyone but Boar. "These two will do. If the payment is sufficient, you can have them back. I'll sell them in two days. On the third day, I'm coming for your settlement. Or you give me my money." Eon made a noise, and Ranger and Sidney were jostled out of the way as four thugs appeared out of nowhere to grab Boar's two extra crewmembers.

There were shouts of protest, but none of them came from Boar.

"Will I have my credits?" Eon asked.

"I guess we'll see in a few days."

Ranger pulled Sidney away then. They didn't need to hear anymore.

13

BOAR WAS A SLAVER.

Boar sold people into *slavery.*

And he did it to provide credits for the upkeep of the settlement.

Sidney stumbled behind Ranger as he led them down the street and away from the slave auction. Her stomach roiled, and she was sure she was about to vomit. Hog and Crow had just been taken as slaves, and Boar had let it happen.

That man, Eon, was coming for the settlement.

They had no way to fight back.

They didn't know danger was coming.

Did they know what Boar did?

If so, Sidney had the urge to let them be taken. It would be retribution for the pain they'd allowed. But the kids in the settlement didn't know. She was sure Cyclone didn't know.

Did the council?

Or did Boar keep his activities a secret?

"We have to warn them." Ranger was a few paces ahead of her, but he heard.

He stopped and turned. "Do you think Boar will make that payment?"

She didn't know her heart could beat this fast. She had to stop walking, or she was going to fall over. Sidney collapsed against a nearby wall, but managed not to slide to the ground. She'd call that a win. "With what credits? The settlement barely has clean water and breathable air. There's no money. We don't even use money! Maybe he could sell the ship, but then the crew would be stranded. Would that even be enough? We don't know how much he owes. And we don't know if that Eon guy will keep his word."

Ranger put his hands on her shoulders and rested his forehead against hers. It felt... good, actually. Really good. Like he was grounding her in the moment. She wanted to wrap her arms around him and hold him close, but she savored the contact he gave her like it was enough.

"We have three days," Ranger pointed out. "And we must be near your settlement. So here's what we're going to do. I'm going to purchase a ship and we're going to go and get everyone in your settlement and take them somewhere safe."

"What? Where?" It was so outlandish that she wanted to laugh. "There are hundreds of people there. How can you even afford a ship that big?" The bigger something was, the more it cost, even Sidney knew that.

Ranger shrugged. "It will be a bit cramped, but we can make it work."

"And where will we take them?" The settlement was a decent chunk of land. It wasn't easy to come by livable terrain, at least that's what the elders said. They couldn't just pick up and find somewhere new.

Now Ranger looked a bit... sheepish. "I have something to confess."

"What? You somehow have access to plenty of land and resources? Who *are* you?" She thought he was just an innocent victim, some spacefaring dragon who'd been at the wrong place at the wrong time.

What other surprises did he have for her?

"I'm a prince. My father is Venin, the Dragon King of Vemion. And I have estates on my home planet more than large enough to handle your settlement, no matter how large." He said it like he was admitting to murder.

"Handle? What do you mean by that? I won't rescue them from one slaver to—" She couldn't let the accusation slip out.

Ranger still looked like she'd slapped him. "Slavery is not tolerated on my planet, and my father punishes slavers harshly."

It was… perfect. Almost too perfect. Ranger was some kind of blessing, and Sidney was scared to believe in him. What if he was lying?

What if he was telling the truth?

"I can't ever repay you for this. Not after what Boar did to you." Ranger didn't need to help her. She wouldn't blame him if he just left her here without a credit to her name. Her people had wronged him atrociously. She'd done the bare minimum to find a way to get him off the ship. "*Why* do you want to help me?"

Ranger stared at her for a long moment, and the silence was so heavy it threatened to make her sink into the dirt. "You need help. I can offer it."

That was the principle that drove most of life on the settlement, but even there it didn't work perfectly. And Sidney wasn't naïve enough to think Ranger was driven by the same ideals. "Why, Ranger?"

He cupped her cheek and kissed her.

Sidney sank into it, loving the feel of his lips against hers. She wanted to feel him naked and pressed against her, sweaty and perfect and *hers*. She could get lost in this kiss, in him.

But she pulled back, unwilling to be deterred. "So you… want me? Is this a trade?" It would be no great sacrifice if that was what Ranger needed to make this even.

But his eyes got big. "No!"

She tried not to feel rejected. "What, then?"

"You need help and I want to help you. Yes, I want you, but if you told me no, I'd still do whatever it took to get your people to safety. Your settlement doesn't deserve the horrors that await them if Boar doesn't come through with his payment. So let me help you. Please." She'd never had a man look at her like that before.

She could get used to it.

Sidney would be in some kind of debt to Ranger forever. She'd owe him not only her life, but the life of every person in the settlement.

And she'd take on the debt. She didn't have another choice.

She only hoped that Ranger was worth it.

"Get the ship. Let's go find my people."

14

To call this an unexpected turn of events would be an understatement. It certainly wasn't how Ranger saw his escape going. Sidney followed along after him, strangely silent. He wanted to hold her hand and kiss her and tell her that everything was going to be alright.

But she was already overwhelmed by his confession about his true identity and the revelation about Boar and his crew. She was entitled to a bit of silence.

Extracting credits was no trouble, but he also had to track down a messaging service to send word back home. He didn't want his father's soldiers flooding into Kalyxia on a hunt for him when he was safely headed home.

Sidney thought she owed him. He'd told her she didn't, but he knew she wouldn't believe that. A lesser man might have gloried in the thought of having his mate in debt to him. It was one way to ensure that she couldn't walk away, not easily at least.

But Ranger didn't want that kind of relationship. He was already a prince, but he wanted a partnership of equals. And he would raise Sidney up until she could stand proudly beside him.

"They just sell ships to anyone?" Sidney asked after a long silence. They'd hired a vehicle to take them to the shipyards, and the dense city was giving way to industrial buildings and factories.

"They'll sell one to me." He wasn't being arrogant. With the number of credits he had and his experience talking his way out of difficult situations, Ranger was sure he could handle one relatively minor transaction.

Sidney was looking out the windows of their transport with poorly disguised awe. "There's only one major road in the settlement. Everything that branches off of it is a pitted pathway. I never realized just how *big* other worlds were."

Ranger bit back his first response. Kalyxia was a backwater, and he had even lower expectations for the other major cities on Kalyx IV. Most of the cities in his kingdom were also small, but that was by design. It allowed dragons to spread their wings and take flight whenever they wanted. No need for cramped, dense populations when there was room enough for all. "Have you wanted to travel?" He didn't want to remind her that she'd probably never see her home again after they rescued her people, so he tried to focus her mind somewhere else.

She shrugged. "I never really thought about it. I've been plenty busy keeping things functioning, and I've been doing enough work for three people. I was so shocked when B—Boar," she said, stumbling a bit over his name, "asked me that I don't think I really had time to be excited. And it's only been a… day, right? My brain is such a mess right now."

"You can rest soon." He couldn't give her anything else, but he could give her that.

She just kept looking out the window.

They pulled into the shipyard, and Ranger's silent prediction held true. Money and the proper attitude were enough to have them outfitted with a ship in under an hour.

The ship was stocked with what they needed. They'd be able to feed a few hundred people for three days, a week if they rationed hard, and Ranger estimated it would be enough time to get them situated back home. The ship's size meant it was docked in orbit, rather than on land, and they had to take a small craft up to their new vehicle.

When Sidney saw it, she gasped and reached for his hand, grasping it hard. If this impressed her, he'd buy her a ship every day.

"Can you fly this thing?" she asked when they entered the main portion of the ship. The mechanics made it a bit loud inside, but it had the echoey feel of an empty room. "That's a bit late to ask, isn't it?"

He laughed. "We've got autopilot. And I'm an adequate pilot myself. We'll manage. But you need to sleep." He put just enough order in his voice to make it clear he wouldn't argue.

"Don't you, too?" She yawned and leaned against the wall.

Ranger needed to find the sleeping quarters before she passed out.

"I'll manage a bit longer. But once we're safely off, I'll be sure to catch a nap," he assured her.

She opened her mouth and then seemed to lose the nerve to say whatever she was planning. "I could use some sleep." She leaned in and kissed his cheek. "Thank you."

He grinned. "You're welcome."

They found the quarters and Sidney sat on the bed, slipping off her shoes in the process. There were more bunks that could fold down the walls, but that wasn't necessary yet.

“Enjoy the room you have to yourself now, we’ll all be sharing soon enough.” He nodded towards the door. “I’ll take the room across the hall. Captain’s quarters. They connect through a hatch to the cockpit." He wanted to invite her to stay with him, but he was no fool. They'd kissed. She was his mate, even if she didn't know it, but the day had been far too eventful for her to deal with any other pressures.

"Okay. Well." She breathed deep and patted her bed. "I'll come find you if I need anything."

And that was his cue to go. "Sleep well." He left her alone.

Exhaustion slammed into him as he walked towards the cockpit, but Ranger had plenty of training to keep himself on his feet. He triple checked the coordinates he entered, just to make sure he wasn't making a mistake, and then they were sailing away from Kalyx IV.

He waited until they were a good distance away from the planet to head back to his own quarters and take a much-needed rest.

He found Sidney waiting for him in his bed.

She blinked the sleep out of her eyes as he entered. "Sorry. Couldn't sleep in the other room."

"You're welcome to m—this bed. I can…"

"Stay with me."

His cock made a valiant effort to rise to the occasion, but tiredness won out. Ranger didn't want to resist the opportunity to feel his mate in his arms. So he simply lifted the blanket and crawled in next to her.

He slept well.

By the time he felt a hand roving over his chest and ducking under his shirt, he was well rested and full of desire. But he held himself still. Those were Sidney's fingers on him. He could feel her breath against his neck.

He wanted more.

He wanted *her*.

But he didn't want to scare her off.

"I can tell you're awake," she whispered against his neck, her lips brushing against his sensitive skin.

He shivered. "Did you sleep well?" It was torture to keep his voice even, but somehow he managed.

"I felt safe with you," was her answer.

He bit back a groan. He wanted her badly. He'd heard of the intensity of the mate bond, but he'd never quite believed it. Not until now. Now he would do anything to have this woman. He'd already thrown his life into upheaval for her. And all she had to do was ask and he'd give her more.

"I want to keep you safe," he said, instead of making confessions that she couldn't yet believe.

Her fingers splayed out, the heat of her skin hot against his own. "Help me forget things. Just for a bit." Her fingers crept to the button of his pants to make clear what she meant.

He rolled over until they were facing one another and captured her mouth with his own. He didn't have the will to resist.

15

SIDNEY WAS FEELING things to a scary degree. Not just betrayal. Not just confusion at the way her life was turned upside down. No, right now she was feeling things for Ranger that she wasn't brave enough to describe. And with his lips pressed against hers, she didn't have to think about it. She could lose herself in this kiss forever.

He rolled them until he was on top of her, one leg in between hers, his knee wedged in between her legs and brushing against her until she squirmed. His hands were tangled in her hair and she was trapped by him.

No, not trapped.

Protected.

Ranger's body was between her and the rest of the universe, and they would have to get through him to get to her. It wasn't fair to him. Getting dependent on this feeling was likely to end in heartbreak. But she could steal these moments for right now.

She wrapped a leg over his hip and pulled his body even closer to her. She could feel the thick length of him through their clothing and wanted to strip bare until she could feel all of him. But getting naked meant ending the kiss, and nothing could pull her lips away from him. Not even air.

He kissed her like she was special. Like this was more than just one stolen moment while their lives intersected.

He kissed her like she belonged to him.

And Sidney wanted that. No one had ever tempted her to wish for something permanent before. And here Ranger was in the space of a day wriggling into her life so deep that she wasn't sure she'd be able to watch him walk away without letting him take a slice of her heart with him.

Pulling away would be the smart move. But Sidney had been smart all her life, and it hadn't gotten her anything but betrayal.

She was taking this time for herself, and she was going to cherish the memory forever.

Ranger undid the buttons of her top with the kind of dexterity that would have made her wonder just how often he did this if she wasn't caught up in the pleasure of his kiss. She made a sound of protest when he pulled away, but then he was pushing her shirt open and exposing her breasts to the cool air of the ship.

"Magnificent," his breath whispered against her skin, making her shiver.

She looked down her body at him, instinct telling her to downplay his words, but his eyes were intent on her and the words caught in her throat. He meant exactly what he said.

And then his lips were on her, tongue laving at her sensitive nipple, and all thoughts of protest were pushed aside. If her breasts were magnificent to see, then his tongue was magnificent to feel.

It was erotic torture, but Sidney didn't want it to end. She squirmed under him, her fingers curling into the sheets and then letting go to grasp him. His own hand was delving into her pants, fingers teasing her moist heat.

Had she ever been this wet before?

What was Ranger doing to her?

She'd had sex before. She'd even enjoyed it. Or so she thought. But it was nothing like this, nothing that made her already crave their next encounter. They were dangerous thoughts circling her brain, but she was powerless to fight them.

She tugged on Ranger until he looked up at her, lips red and wet. She tugged him even harder until they were kissing again. Then she surprised him by arching her hips and sending them rolling so she was straddling his thighs and taking control of the kiss.

He groaned under her and held on as she plundered his mouth. He might have been the dragon, but right then, she was the one who felt powerful. The noises he made were absolutely sinful, and they made Sidney feel like a goddess.

He was her supplicant. Her only priest. And she wanted to reward him for his worship.

She wiggled down his body and almost fell off the bed. It had seemed huge when she laid down beside him, but now that they were moving it seemed not big enough. But she would make do.

She undid his pants and freed his erection, wrapping her fingers around his thick length and stroking.

Ranger groaned again. "Tighter," he gasped out.

She adjusted her grip, but only for a moment. Then she grinned at him and knelt further down to take him into her mouth.

His groan turned into a curse as she swirled her tongue around his head and sucked hard. She wanted to make him beg.

She sank into the pleasure of the act, reveling in her power as Ranger made ridiculous exclamations and promises. She distantly remembered he was a prince and decided that maybe he wasn't kidding when he offered her a pleasure palace of her own.

But that was a promise for another day.

"Mercy, please," he begged, pulling away from her. "Any more and I'm done."

She was sure the smile she gave him was wicked. She felt wicked. "And that's a problem?"

"It is when I haven't tasted you." He reared up and showed her just how much he'd been holding back.

Before she could quite figure out what was going on, Sidney was on her back and her pants were gone as Ranger feasted on her sex, his tongue delving into her and exploring her hidden parts until it was she who was promising him pleasure palaces and other senseless things.

"Inside me, please." She didn't just want his tongue. She wanted his cock inside of her. She wanted to feel joined to him in that most intimate way. The things she felt for him were too intense to explain after such a short acquaintance. But she didn't care.

What she felt was real, even if it dissolved as quickly as it had appeared.

And if it didn't go away…

Well, Sidney would deal with that later.

Ranger hitched her leg up and brushed his thick cock against her entrance. Their gazes locked, and something shifted within her. This was no longer about forgetting her problems, if it ever had been.

This was about letting this thing between her and Ranger burn hot.

He was a dragon. His fire never went out.

He slid into her and it was perfect.

Sensation overtook her, and Sidney surrendered to it. She let her worries fall away as she moved with Ranger. His skin was hot where she gripped him, and though she was probably imagining it, she thought his eyes glowed with fire.

This dragon was everything she could possibly want. And he was satisfying her body in ways she never knew she wanted.

She couldn't let him go.

Ranger thrust into her, and she moaned in pleasure at the way he filled her up. It was exactly what she wanted and so much more. She held onto him hard enough to bruise and wished she could leave a more permanent mark on him. She wanted him to know he was *hers.*

Even if it was only for this moment.

She lost track of time, and her body felt things she didn't know she could feel. It was too much, and yet she still wanted more. What would it take to have this forever?

With a gasp, she started shuddering as an orgasm crested over her, taking her away on a wave of pleasure. Ranger thrust even faster and then he joined her, emptying into her in the primal joining she hadn't known she needed.

They both breathed hard, and Sidney held onto him tight, afraid that if she let him move away, he might disappear.

They floated through space, heading for her settlement, but in that moment, they might have been the only two people in the universe.

16

SIDNEY WASN'T LAYING beside him when Ranger woke up. He wasn't surprised. A small fear lurked in the back of his mind that she would reject him the moment she saw him. That she would tell him it was a mistake to be intimate and he should pretend it never happened.

He'd give her time.

But he wasn't giving up.

He washed quickly and checked the time. They'd be flying into the settlement shortly. And then they'd be flying home. He'd never realized just how much he could miss his own planet. But now he wanted to show it to his mate. He wanted her to love it as much as he did.

Sidney's bedroom door was closed when Ranger stuck his head into the corridor to check. He didn't knock. This was the last time in a long while she'd have time alone, and if she needed to get her thoughts in order, now was the time.

Ranger climbed into the cockpit and read the navigation report. They were less than an hour out, and if the settlement had any sort of defensive scanning equipment, they'd be hailing his ship at any moment.

But the contact never came, and forty-six minutes later, a small dot of a planet showed up on his viewscreen.

Sidney's planet. It didn't have an easy name, just a designation: UF-75X1. According to the fact sheet, it was owned by a mining corporation, and her settlement was listed as a nuisance.

It was no place for a dragon prince's mate.

It was no place for anybody.

The ship was small enough that they'd be able to land on the planet rather than dock in space and ferry passengers to the ship, which was a small mercy. Ranger flicked on the warning signal to let Sidney know it was time to buckle in and prepared to land.

He wasn't much of a pilot. His brother, Saber, used to race through the rocky valleys of the outlands, weaving in and out of dangerous terrain like he was made for it. Ranger had never been brave enough to learn.

Luckily, the piloting required for this mission was straightforward enough.

Sidney met him at the door once they were safely on land. She wore a grim expression, and her bearing was stiff. Ranger wanted to kiss her, or at least hug her. Do something to tell her that everything was going to be alright.

But he had no way to know that. If Eon moved before the deadline, they'd be easy pickings. If Boar came back to warn his people, he'd want to do harm to Sidney. And Ranger, but Ranger didn't care too much for himself when he needed to keep his mate safe.

He wanted off this planet before the sun set. No one could touch them if they were in his kingdom.

"Ready to see my home?" Sidney asked, her voice a bit strained, but brave.

"Absolutely." He couldn't resist reaching out and giving her hand a squeeze, but he dropped it before she could pull away.

He pressed the button to open the door, and a heavy, sulfurous stench filled the cabin. Ranger tried not to grimace, but he wasn't sure he hid his expression well enough.

"It's a byproduct of the mining," Sidney said, taking shallow breaths. "After a bit, you won't even notice it."

He wasn't certain that was a good thing. How could this be safe to breathe?

He was sure he didn't ask that out loud, but Sidney seemed to be reading his mind. "The air scrubbers should take care of most of the stench, but they're malfunctioning. I had to divert power so they make it less toxic. I was hoping to ask Boar—" She choked and it had nothing to do with the air. "Well, I guess that's not going to matter much."

"Where we're going, the air is clean." He meant it as reassurance, but Sidney's shoulders stiffened even further, and she took off on a fast walk, leaving Ranger to catch up.

She walked with easy confidence here, striding down a dirt path towards a collection of buildings that must have been the settlement.

Settlement was a generous term. The dwellings seemed to be half falling over, and he wasn't sure any of the buildings were structurally sound.

It was squalor.

And it shouldn't have been.

Ranger was no expert on the slave market, but he had some idea of what the going prices were and how much it cost to maintain a ship like he'd been held captive on. If Boar and his people provided slaves to Eon or those like him regularly, there should have been more than enough funds to make sure that the settlement was… habitable.

"We should find Cyclone. She'll know what we should do."

What they were going to do was get off the planet as soon as possible and never return. "Are you sure Cyclone isn't working with Boar?"

Sidney glared at him. "Of course. Cyclone would never do that!"

Ranger didn't remind her that she'd thought the same of Boar until a day ago. "We should just round everyone up and get them on the ship. The sooner we're gone the better."

Sidney stopped walking. "About that..."

"What?" Ranger wanted to hurry her on, hoping the stench of the place would be less rank if they were closer to the settlement.

"What if we fortify the settlement? We have an old anti-ship gun that I can rig up. And the miners up the hill have their own defenses. They won't let this place be taken by Eon and his people." She looked hopeful, and Ranger wondered how long she'd been thinking about this.

Or why she'd want to stay.

"I have a feeling the miners would be more than happy for your settlement to be wiped off the planet." His words were harsh, but there was no time for softness. "We don't know what kind of power Eon is bringing with him, but I guarantee he'll be ready to take you all. If you stay here, you're as good as slaves already."

"This is our *home*. Not everyone is going to want to go."

"Then we leave them behind." Hard choices had to be made when enemy fire was incoming; Ranger knew it as well as any warrior.

"I'm not leaving my people behind." Her tone was as strong as stone.

"I'm not letting my mate live in squalor!" It ripped out of him, all of the pressure of the last day or so building up and exploding. He was taking Sidney away to where she would be safe, where she would want for nothing.

"Squalor?" She put her hands on her hips and glared. Then her expression clouded for a moment, and she gave her head a little shake. "Mate?" She was incredulous. "We had sex once, that doesn't make me your mate."

"I recognized you as my mate the moment I saw you. You directed my fire. Sex has little to do with it. You are my mate, Sidney." This wasn't the time to admit it. He'd hoped he could show her his home before he told her, he'd hoped he'd have time to woo her. Instead they were here, and she looked ready to summon his fire and blast him with it.

She opened and closed her mouth several times, as if she was looking for words that wouldn't come.

Finally, she threw her hands up, spun on her foot, and headed towards the village.

"We're talking to Cyclone. If she thinks we can reinforce the settlement, that's what we're doing." She said nothing about being his mate.

Ranger followed after. He'd screwed this up. But he was going to fix it.

He wasn't giving up his mate.

17

MATE. *Dragon* mate. Her?

Squalor.

Ranger was lucky that Sidney didn't have fire powers of her own, or she'd have blasted him with them the moment he'd insulted her home. Sure, it had its shortcomings, but so did every place on the planet.

Even his… palace?

How was she the mate of a dragon prince?

If she thought of it too much, her head was going to explode. She couldn't be his mate. She was just some human foundling who fixed busted machines. She wasn't princess material.

Not that she wanted to be a princess anyway.

She picked up the pace. At this time of day,

Cyclone was likely in her quarters, and she'd know what to do.

Sidney *hoped* that Cyclone would know what to do.

And that she didn't know about Boar's treachery.

People were looking at them strangely as they made it to the heart of the settlement. Ranger looked human when he wasn't in his warrior form, but that didn't matter. He was a stranger. And strangers didn't often come to the settlement.

Sidney picked up the pace, and in a few minutes, they were in front of Cyclone's quarters. Sidney knocked on her door and winced at the warped wood. The door was *fine*. It kept the drafts and weather out.

But Ranger thought she lived in squalor.

Cyclone opened the door and looked between Sidney and Ranger for a moment before beckoning them inside. "It looks like you've got a story to tell."

Some of the tension leaked out of Sidney. Cyclone sounded in good spirits, and if she was on Sidney's side, then the others in the settlement would be too. "This is Ranger," she introduced her... companion. Certainly not her mate. She couldn't deal with that right now. "Ranger, this is Cyclone."

He smiled at Cyclone and gave her a little bow. Any disgust he might have felt at her tiny, slightly dusty dwelling was put away. "It's a pleasure to meet you."

"This boy has manners." Cyclone grinned at Sidney.

Sidney couldn't smile back. "We're in trouble."

Cyclone's expression became serious. "Then I suppose you should both take a seat." She nodded to two sturdy chairs and then sank down onto a pile of pillows she had arranged to her liking. "What's going on?"

Sidney let it all, well, *most* of it out. She told Cyclone about Boar's treachery and Eon's threat. And she let her know there was a ship waiting if they couldn't reinforce the settlement properly.

Ranger stiffened beside her at that last part, but he didn't say anything.

Was he on his best behavior? Or something else?

"I knew that damn fool was going to bring us into his mess someday," Cyclone grumbled. She shifted in her pillows and then stood back up, pacing back and forth. "You say he wanted to sell you in the market?" she asked Ranger.

Ranger nodded.

Why didn't Cyclone sound shocked? Why did she just sound… disappointed?

"Did you know about Boar?" Sidney didn't mean to ask, but the question sort of slipped out.

Cyclone gave her a sad look. "He never said how

he got credits. But there have been whispers for years."

"What? I've never heard anything!" How could Cyclone know and not do anything? How could she stand for this? She was the closest thing that Sidney had to a grandmother *or* a mother, and she'd never said a word.

"You're always with your machines. Machines that require a lot of credits to keep running. I don't condone what Boar does, but..."

Ranger took a deep breath as if he was about to talk, but he said nothing.

Words got tangled up in Sidney's throat. She wanted Cyclone to make it make sense, but she didn't see how it could. So Sidney grabbed her hurt by the throat and pushed it down deep inside of her.

They were on a deadline.

"We need to evacuate." Her words were steady. And there was no longer any chance of fortifying this place, not if people like Cyclone would just go back to turning a blind eye to slavery. "Eon could be here any day now. Boar's probably run away."

"Evacuate?" Cyclone scoffed. "And go where? We're the universe's rejects. Space junk, just like you."

It felt like a knife sinking into her chest. Sidney wasn't junk, even if she'd been discovered in a destroyed ship. "We're people. And Ranger has a place for us."

Cyclone studied Ranger. "This man you say Boar wronged? This man who claims he's a prince? What proof has he given you, girl? He's running a game, and we'll be slaves just the same. Eon isn't taking me alive."

She hadn't heard this tone from Cyclone since she'd been a child, and Sidney didn't like it. "I trust him." Ranger had saved her life more than once. He had no reason to lie.

Except for payback.

It was a niggling doubt, but Sidney pushed it away as well. Ranger had been honest with her.

Except for the mate thing.

And the prince thing.

But he had told her. Eventually.

And she needed to trust someone right now.

"Take it to the council, they can decide what we do next." Cyclone opened the door. "You've never left the settlement before. Maybe you should trust the instincts of your elders."

Sidney stood and refused to meet Cyclone's eyes as she walked out the door.

When they were back on the street, Ranger reached for her hand. "I'm sorry."

She jerked away. "Don't be sorry, be useful." The old adage burst out of her mouth, and she regretted it the moment she said it. It was something Boar used to say when she screwed up as a kid.

"We can try to fortify. It may be best to retreat to the mines, they're likely to be reinforced in some way. And if Eon thinks the place is already abandoned, he may leave without a fight." Ranger offered the suggestion as if it wasn't the antithesis of what he'd said when they'd landed.

Sidney *could* trust him.

He was letting her lead.

"We need to get as many people out of the settlement as possible." She hated that Cyclone and probably some others had an idea of what Boar had been doing. She didn't want to consider if the practice of buying and selling people had started before Boar. But she wasn't going to condemn them to pay for another man's wrongdoings.

They could make up for their own sins once they were safe.

"Hammer."

"What do you need to fix?" Ranger asked.

That made Sidney smile, though it was faint. "We're going to talk to a man named Hammer. He's our best hope."

Hammer slammed the door in her face.

Shadow took one look at Ranger, shook her head, and shooed them away.

Fury said no.

Enigma seemed intrigued, but when Talon shook his head, she changed her mind.

By the time they'd made it through half the village, night was falling and Sidney was close to despair.

And exhaustion.

Her sleep on the ship had been restful, but not nearly long enough. "We can try again in the morning," she told Ranger, leading him back to her quarters. "You can see the squalor I normally live in."

He sucked in a wounded breath. "I'm sorry. I should never have said that."

"You meant it. You don't need to lie." She was just down the street from Cyclone's place, and it was like she'd never left. Of course, it had only been a day and a half or so. She'd been away longer while babysitting the water treatment machine.

Her room wasn't much, but it had been home for years.

"We'll make more progress in the morning," he said, with the kind of confidence she wished she had.

Sidney sank down into her bedding and then pulled the blanket back. "I've only got the one blanket."

"Are you sure?"

"Come cuddle with me, dragon prince." He was the only thing that felt right anymore.

Ranger came and cuddled.

She could have asked him about the mate stuff. He would probably even tell her, but Sidney kept her mouth shut. She wasn't sure she wanted to know. There'd be time to ask later, when they weren't balanced on the edge of danger.

That was her last thought as she fell asleep.

A few hours later, a harsh beeping pulled her from slumber, and Ranger stiffened beside her.

"What's that?" she mumbled, sleep heavy in her voice.

Ranger was wide awake and grim. "I tasked sensors from my own planet to scan for Eon's fleet. That's confirmation that they're headed our way."

"How long?" She looked out the window, but the sky was dark and full of stars. Not a spaceship in sight.

"Half a day at most."

"We need to move."

They got up. They could sleep when they were free.

18

THE SUN WAS ONLY BEGINNING to break over the horizon, but people in the settlement were working. There was a line out the door at Shadow's kitchen, and Sidney could hear the sounds of construction echoing down the street.

There was no hint that a slaver ship was almost there. No hint that the settlement would be dead come nightfall, one way or another.

"What do you think?" Ranger asked as Sidney surveyed the street.

They'd gone to everyone likely to help the day before and found no success. Sidney felt even more urgency than yesterday, but the other residents of the settlement had no reason to.

"We try Cyclone again. And if that doesn't work, we make an announcement of what's coming. We save who we can." Her heart was heavy, and she feared she'd be the only one leaving.

How could she even consider it? These were her people, her *family.* And they were in more danger than they'd ever been in.

But she knew that Eon was coming, and she couldn't sacrifice herself, not like that. She wouldn't be a slave.

Was kidnapping the entire settlement for their own good an option? She eyed Ranger. He had those nifty fire powers.

Maybe *that* was the last resort.

Cyclone was tending to the dusty patch of sad flowers in front of her dwelling when Ranger and Sidney got there. She gave Ranger a glare and Sidney a pitying look. "I said what I meant to say."

"The slaver that Boar owes money to is going to be here sometime today. Ranger's security sensors detected his presence. We have a ship that can fit everyone in the settlement, and he has a place where we can safely settle. Please, Cyclone. Help us." Sidney's voice didn't shake, and she was proud of that. But she could already see that she hadn't gotten through.

"I've lived here for seventy years. I'm not running." Her gnarled fingers gripped a small, rusted spade.

"Please, you have—"

Ranger put a hand on her arm. "We must respect our elders," he said, cutting her off.

Sidney looked at him, face scrunched in confusion and anger simmering. She was ready to turn her ire and frustration on him when he kept talking to Cyclone.

"Madam, I have only been with Sidney for a couple of days, but I can see the values that you have imparted on her. I apologize for our abruptness, and that we did not seek more of your counsel last night."

Where was *this* coming from? Ranger was speaking like some sort of robot, and it was so out of character—as far as she knew—that she was shocked into silence.

"Sidney says you've been pivotal in the running of this settlement, and that is no easy feat. It makes you more of a leader than I've ever been. My brother will hold the throne one day. I have no desire to be anyone's king. But I beg you to reconsider." He pulled out a small communicator and handed it to her. "This is the information I've managed to gather from my kingdom's files on the slaver Eon. He has done this before, and he will likely succeed here. If you still want to stay once you've read the file, then you stay. But please at least consider our proposition." He gave her a slight bow and pulled Sidney back towards the road.

"What in all the stars was *that*?" Sidney demanded once they were out of earshot.

"Diplomacy." Ranger walked slowly and kept distance between them. "She needs to come to the decision herself. And it never hurts to lay on a bit of flattery."

"Who *are* you?" She'd seen him act as a warrior from the moment they'd met, not a diplomat, and it made her wonder what other facets he was hiding.

He grinned at her, and it did something to her insides.

She couldn't fall for him. It would be so stupid. He was a prince, she was just a mechanic.

But...

"What's this mate thing all about?" she gathered up the courage to ask.

Ranger grinned even broader. "It's—"

"Come back here this instant!" Cyclone summoned them with a forceful shriek.

Sidney and Ranger hurried back. Cyclone had gone pale, and her hand was shaking as she handed the communicator back to Ranger. "How certain are you of what that says?"

"Dead certain," Ranger said gravely.

"Then we need to leave. Let's go." Cyclone spared a glance at her dwelling, but didn't go inside for anything. There wasn't room for many sentimental items in the settlement.

With Cyclone's support, Sidney and Ranger had the success they'd failed to grab the night before. Cyclone gave orders, and everyone jumped to follow. She was commanding that way.

"I'll go power up the ship so we're ready as soon as the last person is on board," Ranger told her as Cyclone explained the situation to a group outside of Shadow's kitchen.

Everyone was getting out. Things were going to be okay.

And Ranger was doing it all for her.

Sidney grabbed Ranger's shirt and pulled him close, giving him a brief—but thorough—kiss in front of the entire settlement. Distantly she heard someone whoop, but she was too caught up in the sensation of Ranger's lips against her to care who it was.

When she pulled back, Ranger was smiling. "I'm going to keep you, Sidney mine."

She gave him another quick kiss before forcing herself to take a step back. "Go start the ship, dragon prince."

Ranger left.

It wasn't an orderly evacuation. There wasn't a procedure to get the entire settlement off the planet in a matter of hours, and they had to find a way to account for everyone. There was no official census to keep track of who lived in the settlement, but they were only a few hundred people. Everyone knew everyone else.

"How are we doing?" she asked Cyclone after they'd sent a large group to join Ranger at the ship.

"Four unaccounted for. Hammer has gone out to find them. I told him to be back at the ship in an hour, with or without them. We're running out of time."

That was true. Every second counted, and Sidney kept imagining Eon's ship appearing on the horizon. Her heart was beating fast, and the heat wasn't the only reason she was sweating.

They did a sweep of the settlement to make sure no one was hiding away. It was a ghost town, and a part of Sidney wanted to cry at the loss. She'd lived her whole life here. This was home.

And she'd never see it again.

Even if the threat from Eon was gone, she didn't know how she could go back.

"How sure are you of Ranger?" Cyclone asked as they finished their sweep and started back towards the ship.

"As sure as I can be. He is who he says he is."

"I hope you're right." If Cyclone was doubtful, it wasn't stopping her from moving.

They could hear the rumbling engines of the ship before it came into sight. Sidney let out a relieved sigh. They were almost done. They were almost safe.

Then the piercing shriek of an alarm knocked her a step back and almost pushed Cyclone to the ground.

Something was wrong.

They ran.

19

THE PROXIMITY ALARM SHOUTED, and Ranger had to act. The ship was crawling with people from the settlement. But Sidney wasn't back.

He wasn't leaving without her.

He wanted to rush off the ship to find her, but he'd promised her that he would get her people to safety. So he would keep his promise… as long as it meant not abandoning her.

The warning system showed a large ship within fighting distance of the planet. There was a small chance the craft was headed towards the mine and didn't care about the settlement, but Ranger wasn't willing to risk it.

This was Eon.

Ranger's ship didn't have much offensive capability. There were small lasers and it was small enough to be nimble, but they'd have to rely on his piloting skills, rudimentary as they were, and the ship's defensive shield.

He put in a call to the Vemion Planetary Defense with a warning that he was incoming and would have an enemy on his tail. He just had to survive long enough so that his own forces could overwhelm Eon.

"Strap in," he commanded over the loudspeaker. "Prepare for takeoff. Hostile incoming."

Where was Sidney?

She'd stayed behind with Cyclone to make sure that she could save as many people in the settlement as possible. It was admirable. But he'd much rather admire her while she was on his damn ship. She was supposed to check in once she was on board and clear him for takeoff.

She hadn't checked in.

He wasn't cleared.

The alarm kept blaring. They were running out of time.

He cycled through the viewscreens to see that the settlers were strapping in. Most of them were following orders, but a few seemed to be arguing amongst themselves.

"If you're not strapped in, takeoff may kill you," he barked out over the intercom. There was no time for gentle cajoling.

A few of the arguers sat down.

Ranger eyed the control that would close the main door and seal the ship. They'd need to seal in a couple of minutes before takeoff to ensure correct pressurization and let life support adjust.

The ship on the security screen was getting closer. Estimated time of arrival was fifteen minutes.

Ranger's fire raged inside of him. He felt powerful enough to blast the ship from orbit with his own flames. But there were too many lives at stake for him to test that hypothesis.

No one harmed his mate.

He was about to unstrap and run out to find Sidney when the ship beeped and the doors closed.

"I'm on board," Sidney's voice crackled over the intercom. "What's happening?"

It was a private message between her radio and his, not broadcast for the rest of the passengers. "Eon's almost here. We lift off in five minutes."

"I'm coming to you."

He would have understood if she wanted to sit with her people, but he was grateful for her presence beside him. "Your seat is waiting." If this was the end, he wanted to be near his mate.

The ship was large enough that it took Sidney almost the whole five minutes of pre-takeoff to reach him. Ranger had just warned the passengers to strap in or die when the door opened and she burst in.

She was breathing hard, and there was a smudge of dirt on her face. He'd never seen a more beautiful sight.

"Hammer found them. We got everyone." She sounded more exhausted then relieved.

Ranger would have spared her a moment for congratulations, but it was time to lift off. "Strap in. We're going home."

She did.

With a final prayer and a hope that Vemion forces were waiting for them, Ranger lifted off.

They climbed easily, cutting through the air like it was nothing. The ship rocked as they broke through the atmosphere, and the viewscreen darkened as day gave way to the eternal night of space.

The proximity alarm had been quiet while Ranger prepared for takeoff, but the moment they were out of the planet's orbit, it started blaring again, even louder than before.

And the reason became obvious within a minute. Eon wasn't fifteen minutes out. He was right there and waiting.

The defensive shields took the brunt of laser fire that shot from Eon's ship. He shouldn't have known that Ranger and Sidney were ferrying the settlement to safety, but he must have had intel of his own.

Even though it didn't do much, Ranger shot a thin

stream of laser fire back at Eon. It was a distraction, if nothing else.

"Hold on," he warned his mate.

"I trust you." She sounded sure.

He had to prove it to her.

A skilled pilot could nimbly fly this ship in circles. Ranger was competent… at best. And he didn't need to evade Eon forever, just for long enough. So rather than do anything tricky, he punched in the coordinates for Vemion and pointed the ship in the right direction, putting all the power and speed they could muster into it.

Eon shot an even stronger blast of lasers at them, and the defensive system barked a warning. "System damaged, defenses at 70%."

A second jolt of lasers knocked their systems down to 63%.

"Are we—" Sidney cut off her own question, and Ranger couldn't even spare her a glace or a reassuring nod.

They needed more speed. They were at the max safe limit, but that wasn't all the ship could do.

He put in the override on their speed modulator. The screen flashed all kind of warnings, but Ranger ignored them. They couldn't take much more from the blasters.

Another jolt and the defense system dropped to 59%.

They were close to Vemion. The two planets were in the same system, and patrols circled far, especially when they knew there was a prince in need of help. But how close?

"If I divert the power from auxiliary life support, I can get us a bit more speed. But if anything happens to the main system, we're dead." He wasn't asking Sidney for permission, not exactly, but he couldn't bring himself to make that final call.

"How close are we to your planet?" she asked. She reached out and placed her hand over his, offering him a bit of comfort.

"Not close enough."

The ship jolted as another laser shot rocked them. Defenses at 57%.

"We're not taking as much damage," Sidney pointed out. "There must be some distance between us."

Ranger confirmed that with a look at one of his nav screens. "For now."

She squeezed his hand. "Divert the power."

He did it. And then he laced their fingers together as they used the last of the available power to put on a burst of speed. Any faster, and they'd be in danger of overshooting Vemion, and they couldn't risk that.

He didn't let go of Sidney's hand, and she clung to him like he was a lifeline. But they didn't say anything to each other.

"We have you on our sensors, your highness. Support incoming."

Ranger almost didn't believe it when the call came over the system. Then he let out a whoop of joy and kissed Sidney's hand. If they weren't flying so fast, he would have unbuckled himself and kissed her.

Two Vemion defense vessels zoomed past them and started shooting. Ranger let them handle Eon.

It was time to show Sidney his home.

20

SIDNEY GOT her first glimpse of Vemion through the view screen just a few minutes later. It didn't look real. From space, the planet looked like a blue jewel that couldn't possibly be home to people. But from the smile that crept onto Ranger's face, it was.

He put the ship down in a busy shipyard, and things got crazy after that. Dozens of people surrounded the ship and started rushing passengers off. There was a tent set up on the far end of the yard where it looked like medics were checking people over, and another group of people with clipboards were taking their information.

"What is all of this?" Sidney asked before she could be pulled away from Ranger. She wanted to grip his hand and stay close. Everything on this planet was bright and blue and clean. She was afraid if she stopped looking at Ranger, it would all dissolve into a dream.

"My position has its benefits." He reached for her.

She was reaching back when a young woman ran up to them. "Please, miss, I need to get your information. My name is Cal." Cal looked at Ranger, and her eyes widened, then she gave him a short bow. "Your highness."

So the prince thing was real. Not that Sidney really doubted it.

"Go," Ranger urged. "I need to explain this all to my father before he hears it from someone else. May I come to you later?"

Sidney managed a nod. Her dragon prince mate was going to talk to his dragon king father. It was a bit much to take in.

Ranger smiled and gave her a quick kiss before running off.

Cal made a shocked noise.

Sidney wasn't interested in long explanations. "Let's get me processed."

There was a medical check, and then she was ferried to one of the clipboard wielding dragons to have all of her information taken down. After that, Sidney weaved in and out of her people, checking on them and assuring them that everything would be fine.

She found Cyclone after a bit. "What do you think?" she asked. She was trying not to sound smug.

"Let's see where they take us after this," was Cyclone's reply. But she sounded more curious than doubtful.

One of the settlement's children, Nightowl, came up to Sidney with tears in her eyes. She reached her hands out and Sidney picked her up, setting her on her hip. "You're getting a bit big, little bird." She hugged the child tight.

"I'm scared," Nightowl whispered like it was a shameful secret.

"We're safe now." Sidney hoped the child believed her. "Ranger made sure of it."

"You made sure of it," Cyclone said. "Now give me that child. You've got a man to find."

Sidney wanted to protest, but Nightowl went freely into Cyclone's arms and Sidney was left alone. She talked to more people from the settlement, and the mood seemed optimistic, if a bit wary.

Cal found her. "We've prepared temporary quarters for everyone. I'm having transportation brought around. Are you ready to go?"

Sidney wanted to tell Cal that she wasn't in charge, but already her people were looking at her expectantly. Even the council members in charge of keeping the settlement running weren't trying to take control. That would change, she was certain. And it wasn't like she *wanted* to be in charge. But if people were willing to follow her today, she would lead them.

"I think we're ready."

It took hours to get everyone settled in. They were in what appeared to be repurposed soldiers' barracks, stuffed between two buildings that weren't quite meant to hold as many people as they were. Cal assured Sidney it would only be for a few days until his highness could secure the proper lodgings in one of his territories.

His highness.

Territories.

Sidney was a bit lightheaded thinking about it.

She was starting to wonder if he would come back. He'd been gone for hours by now. She'd even been assigned her own bed in the barrack. Cal had gone off with all the other dragon helpers on a mission to outfit everyone with new clothes and get them fed.

Ranger was probably busy.

What if his father sent them away?

The thought knocked her back a bit. If Eon was captured, wasn't it safe to go back? The threat from Boar's wrongdoing was taken care of.

Back to their home right under the mine, where the water was dirty and the air smelled of chemicals.

Where their livelihood, for whatever it was worth, was financed by the bondage of strangers.

All of that, to live in squalor.

Sidney didn't want to go back. She didn't know what life held for them here, but she wanted it to be better.

Boar was still out there somewhere. And if they returned to the settlement, he'd still be a threat.

But that wasn't the real reason she wanted to stay.

A hush fell over the barrack, and it became obvious why when Ranger walked between the two rows of bunks and stopped in front of her. He'd changed his clothes from the outfit he'd been wearing since they'd met. Now he wore a fine jacket with golden embroidery on the rich, blue fabric and tight pants that would have told her just how fine his ass was if she hadn't already seen it for herself.

He held out his hand.

She took it.

They left the barracks on a wave of silence.

Sidney was probably going to have questions to answer. Later.

"I want to show you my home," Ranger said.

"I want to see it." What she'd seen of his planet was already enough to have her grateful. It was impossible to imagine there was more.

But he was a dragon prince.

And she could almost believe that she really was his mate.

They rode a small vehicle, and Sidney was too focused on the scenery passing by to say much. It was so *green*. And the sky was so blue. Ranger was content to just sit beside her.

They stopped in front of a huge stone building, and Sidney's first instinct was to wonder if this was a city.

"It's not as overwhelming when you're inside," Ranger assured her.

"All this house for one person."

"It's for anyone in the family. But I have primary use of it. And the servants, of course." He tugged her out of the vehicle.

Of course.

If she'd thought she was in over her head, now she was sure of it.

Ranger didn't head for the entrance of the house, instead following a small gravel path around the side to an opening in the verdant hedge. And once they were through, it was like stepping into *another* new world, one of flowers and butterflies and small birds.

There was nothing like this back at the settlement. She wasn't sure there was another place anywhere like it in the galaxy.

"This is why I make this house my home. They could tear down the house, and as long as the garden remained, I'd stay here." He led her down the paths, pointing out some of his favorite flowers.

Eventually Sidney started to relax. It was a beautiful garden. And it showed her another aspect of Ranger she couldn't have imagined. She started asking questions: the name of a flower, how he'd come to love this place, anything that came to mind. And he answered freely.

She wasn't sure how long they talked, but the sky was starting to darken by the time he pointed to a small bench and asked if she wanted a rest.

"Do you like it?" he asked carefully. This place was special to him.

"It's the most beautiful thing I've ever seen. Of course I do." But it was just more proof she was out of place.

"Sid—"

"I'm space trash." He had to know the truth about her before this went any further.

His eyes crinkled in confusion. "What?" He wasn't backing away. Not yet.

The story would come out eventually. Everyone in the settlement knew her story, and if they saw her palling around with a prince, the rumor was sure to spread.

"I'm not even really from the settlement. They found me in a debris field when I was only a few months old. Somehow, I'd been put in a survival suit.

Cyclone was the one that found me. They brought me to the settlement and raised me among the other children. But I don't know who my parents are or where I'm really from. They could have been slavers. Or pirates. Something terrible." It was a fear that lived deep inside of Sidney. Most of the other children of the settlement at least knew their background, even if their people had come to the settlement after being rejected elsewhere.

She didn't have that.

"You're not trash." Ranger still wasn't backing away. "And I don't care who your parents were. I care for you. I know it's a lot, my position and all of this. And I know we've only just met. But I want you to give me the chance to court you as a mate should, to prove to you that I'm worth the trouble." Fire swirled in his eyes, and Sidney could almost feel it.

She looked at the towering edifice of his house. This was the kind of trouble that she'd never thought to prepare for. And yet…

"You saved my people. You look like *that*. And you shared your garden. Do you really think I'm not already halfway there?" Before he could respond, she leaned in and kissed him.

Being a dragon's mate was going to take some getting used to.

But she'd figure it out if it meant she got to keep Ranger.

21

EXCITEMENT HUMMED in Ranger's veins as he led Sidney into his house and towards his chambers. It was good to be home. And even better to have his mate at his side.

"I can have a room made up for you," he forced himself to offer. After her kiss, his body was ready for more, but he couldn't assume. He hadn't earned the right.

Sidney squeezed his hand. "I want to see your room."

That was answer enough.

He pointed out the art fixtures on the walls and explained the history of this wing of the house. It meant they moved slower, and he realized he was deliberately delaying to build anticipation.

Sidney realized it too. "Ranger?"

"Yes?"

"Give me the tour later."

Her wish was his command. He sped up, his long strides making it so that Sidney almost had to jog to keep up. It startled a laugh out of her, and he swept her up into his arms and ran the final distance, signaling the motion sensor to open the door to his quarters.

The large windows let in the fading light, and if Sidney looked, she'd see what his room looked like, but her eyes were trained on him.

He couldn't look away from her.

Every piece of furniture could have been painted purple and hung from the ceiling and Ranger wouldn't have noticed, so long as his bed was where it belonged and Sidney was in his arms.

He set her down gently on the soft mattress.

"I'm not going to break," she told him, her hand running over the silk of the sheets.

"That doesn't mean you shouldn't be taken care of." He wanted to worship her, wanted her to know that she owned him completely. His mate was nothing like he'd expected and yet everything he could ever hope to want.

And he had her in his bed.

He was a lucky dragon.

"Take off your clothes." If he got a hand on her, he feared he'd summon his claws and tear them off. He wanted to see her bare in his bed. He wanted to bury himself inside of her until he didn't know where he ended and she began.

"Oh, so now you're giving orders?" she teased. But she pulled her shirt off regardless.

"Only the ones you'll bless me with following." His eyes were caught on the way the light hit her skin, almost making it glow. She'd look glorious bathed in his fire, and he wanted to see it one day.

He took off his own clothes and joined her on the bed. He let his hands trace where the light touched her and watched as she shivered, her skin pebbling under his fingers. She gasped as he moved his hand to cup her breast, thumb brushing against her nipple just long enough to bring it to a peak.

He replaced his thumb with his lips, letting his tongue do the work to bring her this pleasure.

Her hands roved over his naked skin, and Ranger felt anchored to her, just where he belonged.

He gave his attention to her other breast, unwilling to neglect any part of her. She writhed under him, and he wanted her begging.

So he moved lower.

When he set his mouth on her sex, she let out a creative curse that almost had him pulling away... until her fingers dug into his hair and held him in place. She may have been letting him do what he wanted, but she was by no means a passive partner in this dance.

He savored the taste of her. This was his mate, all hot and wet around him, the one person in the universe truly meant for him. And he planned to live a good portion of his life between her thighs. It was his privilege and his duty.

While his tongue worked her nub, he let his fingers delve into her wet heat, stretching and stroking until her hips jerked and humped against him. Oh yes, this was exactly where he wanted to be.

His cock was hard and desperate for release, but Ranger summoned all the control he could. He was here to give his mate pleasure. His cock would have to wait.

Just a bit.

He wasn't about to torture himself.

And when Sidney rippled around him and called out his name, he felt the kind of triumph that normally only came on the battlefield. But this kind of victory was one they could both enjoy.

While she was still gasping, Ranger moved, positioning his cock at her entrance and slowly easing his way into her. Sidney grabbed one of his hands and laced their fingers together.

They were already connected so intimately, but somehow her grip made it even better.

And then he was inside of her, and she was

squeezing tight around him. He could get lost in the feel of her, and he did, letting himself sink into the sensation and letting everything else fall away until it was just him, and her, and the feel of their bodies linked together.

Then he moved.

The slide of his flesh inside of her was its own kind of torture, one Ranger would gladly submit to until the end of time. He summoned all his strength and discipline, unwilling to let this be finished before his mate was satisfied.

He could feel in the press of her body and hear in the noises she made that she was close. He moved faster, trying to find the spot to hit just right that would make her see stars.

And he did. She gasped and her hips jerked. Her hand spasmed, and she let go of him, her fingers curling into the sheets as he gave her exactly what she craved.

They moved in unison until Sidney called out his name and her pleasure crested once more. It was too much for Ranger, with the way her body clung to his, and he let himself go, emptying inside of her and finishing exactly where he belonged.

They both took their time to recover, but even as his cock slid out of her, Ranger couldn't let Sidney go completely.

"Will it always feel like this?" Sidney asked him

with a kind of vulnerability he knew to cherish. She was a woman who knew how to protect herself, but she was letting him close to her heart. Close enough that one day he might take it for himself.

It was only fair. She already owned his.

"It's only going to get better." The fire of their mate bond was hot, and it was a blaze that Ranger planned to stoke forever.

"You promise?"

"You have my word." And a dragon prince never went back on his word. He hoped that as Sidney grew to knew him, she'd know that.

"I'm going to keep you," she muttered as she surrendered to sleep.

Ranger smiled and held her closer. Finally, everything was right. And for the first time in days, he let himself drift off into a restful sleep, putting all his worries aside. He was home. He had his mate.

He was ready to face anything.

EPILOGUE

THREE WEEKS later

"Be careful with that! If you break it, the whole construction project is going to be set back another week!" Sidney watched as two of her people placed one of the machines they'd need to build their housing structures.

Three weeks in the barracks was more than enough time to make her people certain they wanted places of their own. Competently building houses was another matter.

"They do know we have professional construction crews available, right?" Ranger walked down the path and put an arm around her when they were close enough to touch.

Sidney loved it. They couldn't keep their hands off one another, something that had almost gotten them in trouble on more than one occasion. She didn't ever want it to stop.

"They need to do it themselves. It's hard to start over." Privately, she agreed that professionals would be helpful, but it wasn't going to happen.

"They're making headway, at least." Ranger kissed her cheek.

None of her people even looked their way. They were used to it by now.

Ranger had found the land for them and negotiated terms with the council. Each former resident of the settlement would owe him a set amount of labor every year. Other than that, they were free to do what they wanted. Ranger had confessed to her that he'd be happy to give them the land outright, but Sidney knew her people.

They needed the agreement he'd offered. He'd already done so much for them, and they needed to give something back.

She heard little footsteps running their way right before the hiccupping breath of a crying child. She was ready to lift little Nightowl into her arms, but the girl went straight to Ranger, who bent down and lifted her up like it was the most natural thing in the world.

"What's wrong, little one?" he asked in a soft voice, cradling the girl gently and rocking her a bit to calm her down.

Apparently, his dragon powers also had the power to calm children. At least, that's what Sidney was attributing it to. She'd never calmed a kid that fast. And she *wasn't* jealous.

Or charmed.

Who was she kidding? Seeing Ranger take care of a kid was doing all kinds of things to her insides.

Nightowl explained whatever the issue was to Ranger, and he listened to her just as intently as if he were talking to the king.

"Do you want me to carry you over there? Or can you walk?" he asked her.

Nightowl scrunched her face up. "Walk," she finally decided.

Ranger put her down, but the little girl gripped his hand so he couldn't get away from her.

Sidney could relate.

Her mate leaned in and kissed her quickly. "Excuse me, my love. I must go tend to the little owl's issue."

Sidney let him go, even as her heart flipped over.

Oh yeah, she'd definitely chosen right when she chose Ranger.

Once she accepted the mating, it was the easiest thing in the world. The dragon prince stuff? That was taking some getting used to. Ranger's father, King Venin, was a bit terrifying. And she was pretty sure he didn't like her.

Too bad. She wasn't going anywhere.

She saw Ranger deliver Nightowl to a group of other children and then get pulled into some kind of game with them and smiled.

She was exactly where she belonged.

Thank you for reading *Ranger*!

I'd appreciate it so much if you would consider leaving a review.

The series continues with *Saber*.

WHAT'S TO READ NEXT: SABER

Prince Saber's made a huge mistake.

When his father commands him to marry a dragon lady, Saber agrees. But once he meets Lady Mirage, he fears he's made the biggest blunder of his life.

But there's more to Lady Mirage than it seems. And when they escape the expectations of the Dragon Kingdom Saber wonders if Mirage is a mistake… or a miracle.

Check it out!

INTERGALACTIC DATING AGENCY

LOOKING for love that's out of this world? These strong, smart, sexy aliens are seeking mates from the Milky Way. Just hop onboard with your local Intergalactic Dating Agency. Join our group of authors as we explore the friendly skies and beyond with trilogies of cosmic craving, astral adventure, and otherworldly lovers. Warning: abductions may or may not be included!

ALSO BY KATE RUDOLPH

Looking for something else? Kate Rudolph has a heart pounding collection or paranormal and sci-fi romance stories for you! Bundles, bears, audiobooks, aliens, and more. Check out your options in the list below. You can find out all you need to know at www.katerudolph.net.

Want to check out one of the books? Click on the series name to find out more!

Dragon Brides

Fated mates, fierce women, and dragon princes.

Crux

Ranger

Saber

Zulir Warrior Mates

Kidnapped humans. Alien Warriors. Electric wings.

The Zulir Warrior Mates series brings you human heroines

and heroes abducted from Earth who find love – and wings! – with the alien warriors who rescue them.

Also available in audio!

Synnr's Saint

Synnr's Hope

Synnr's Spark

Synnr's Kiss

Guarded by the Shifter

Werewolf. Bodyguard. Mate.

The origins of these shifters are shrouded in mystery, but they're determined to protect their mates from any harm that comes their way.

Also available in audio!

Hunting Season

On the Prowl

Stalking Magic

Detyen Warriors

Detya was destroyed a hundred years ago. These

doomed warriors are out to find justice… and their mates.

The Detyen Warriors series brings you kick butt heroines, alpha alien heroes, fated mates, and relationships strong enough to span the galaxy!

The entire series is also available in audio!

Soulless

Ruthless

Heartless

Faultless

Endless

Alien Holiday Romance

Christmas… in space????

These alien holiday romances look beyond Earth's winter holidays and ring in the season across the galaxy! ***Select titles available in audio.***

Snowed in with the Alien Beast

The Alien's Winter Gift

The Alien Reindeer's Wild Ride

Trapped with her Alien Mate

Alien Outlaws

Outlaws, schemes, and love… it's all there in the Alien Outlaws series…

Andie Munster is sick of life on Ixilta, the planet she got dumped on after being abducted from Earth six years ago. And when the mysterious and dangerous Xandr shows up looking for a way off the planet, she's half-prisoner, half-co-conspirator in a wild rush to escape.

Rogue Alien's Escape

Rogue Alien's Woman

Rogue Alien's Secret

Rogue Alien's Legacy

Mated to the Alien

Fated Mate Alien Romance

Detyens are doomed to die young if they don't find their fated mates.

Follow along as these mated pairs fight off aliens, corrupt dictators, prejudiced humans, pirates, and more! The books can be read or listened to in any order, though some characters show up in multiple stories.

Select books available in audio.

Pick a book and jump into the action today!

Ruwen

Tyral

Stoan

Cyborg

Krayter

Kayleb

Shayn

Braxtyn

Doryan

Dekon

Stealing the Alpha

The thief takes what she wants, but the alpha keeps what's his...

Join shifter thief Mel as she clashes with lion alpha Luke in an explosive trilogy of two opposites who can't keep away from one another.

Also available in audio!

The Alpha Heist

Entangled with the Thief

In the Alpha's Bed

Save with box sets!

Aliens. Shifters. Warriors. Mates. Get them all wrapped together in these special box sets. Save up to 30% off the price of buying the individual books, depending on the series!

Alien Outlaws: The Complete Series

Mated to the Alien Volume One (also available in audio)

Mated to the Alien Volume Two (also available in audio)

Mated to the Alien Volume Three

Mated to the Alien Volume Four

Stealing the Alpha: The Complete Series (also available in audio)

The Mate Bundle

Detyen Warriors Volume One (also available in audio)

Detyen Warriors Volume Two (also available in audio)

Zulir Warrior Mates Volume One (also available in audio)

Standalone Paranormal and Sci-Fi Romance:

Crashed

Mated on the Moon

Mated to the Alien Dragon

Marked

Bear in Mind

Alpha's Mercy

Gemma's Mate

Find more by Kate Rudolph at www.katerudolph.net

ABOUT KATE RUDOLPH

Kate Rudolph is a paranormal and alien romance author who lives in Indiana. She loves writing about kick butt heroines and the steamy heroes who love them. She's been devouring romance novels since she was too young to be reading them and had to hide her books so no one would take them away. She couldn't imagine a better job in this world than writing romances and sharing them with her fellow readers.

If you enjoyed this story, please consider leaving a review.

www.ingramcontent.com/pod-product-compliance
Lightning Source LLC
La Vergne TN
LVHW051002080826
845145LV00009B/2408